FOREVER ENDEAVOR

MISSION 16

BLACK OCEAN: PASSAGE OF TIME

J.S. MORIN

Magical Scrivener Press
www.magicalscrivener.com

Publisher's Note: This is a work of fiction. Names, characters, places, and incidents are a product of the author's imagination. Locales and public names are sometimes used for atmospheric purposes. Any resemblance to actual people, living or dead, or to businesses, companies, events, institutions, or locales is completely coincidental.

Ordering Information: Special discounts are available on quantity purchases by corporations, associations, and others. For details, contact the publisher at the address above.

J.S. Morin — First Edition

FOREVER ENDEAVOR
MISSION 16

DEEP beneath the city of New Vancouver, the living heart of the Martian Military Government skipped a beat. The declaration of martial law had been a formality, the mere dropping of a flimsy pretense. An evacuation of senior officials had been a mainly z-axis maneuver. Everyone important that could be rounded up on short notice—and who hadn't already fled early on in the crisis—had been gathered here, in this nameless emergency bunker not far from the civic center.

Eric had been caught in that wide net. And it had been three days now that he'd been impersonating Vice Admiral Stuart "Stooie" Quatermain before a gaggle of his supposed peers.

And each of those three days had started the same: with a briefing.

Day by day, it seemed, Eric started the briefing farther from the end where General Bob held court.

"Elections. Fucking *elections!*" the supreme leader of Mars bellowed. "They try to blow up our planetary nominating convention, and they have the *gall* to announce elections of their own?"

Eric studied his coffee, which was hard because it was plain black coffee of the sort they give soldiers in the field, filled with sciencey goo to keep it from spoiling. He'd forgone a chemical sweetener he couldn't pronounce and a form of powdered "cream" with an expiration date he'd be lucky to outlive. While all the additives *might* have made it worthy of a second look, it kept him from daring to drink it.

Sure, maybe he *looked* like Stooie Quatermain, but he was still Eric Ramsey. He had his health to consider.

"What if we got them back in kind?" Admiral Hershey suggested. "You know, send some spooks their way, even if it doesn't amount to much?"

Admiral Fallon scoffed openly. "After that wizard barbecued two-thirds of Earth's senate already? We'd look like the runt who comes over to kick a dead body his gang buddies just ventilated."

"In that case, why not just park our whole fleet in orbit and demand they turn over Tiffany Bell?"

There was a moment of expectant silence. Furtive eyes turned Eric's way. It took a hasty recreation in the Village of Eternity, consulting the real Stooie Quatermain's mind to determine the reason. Apparently, the vice admiral Eric inhabited had once pulled the maneuver described on a border colony that had sabotaged one of his shuttles while his subordinates were taking shore leave. But he hadn't accounted for the colony having real orbital defenses, and he'd been forced to withdraw ingloriously.

"Wasn't funny then. Isn't funny now," he moped, trying to mimic Stooie Quatermain's reaction in the recreation of this same bunker in the Village.

"Leave Stooie out of this," General Bob barked. "Last thing

we need is dead-end trips down nostalgia lane. Earth's not looking which way they're punching, and we need to spot the opening for a snapback."

One thing Eric had been picking up on had been the supreme general's boxing analogies. Unfortunately, among the varied personas dwelling in his mind, knowledge of the sport was scattershot, conflicting, and sparse. Colonial adaptations, alien influences, and holo-sport modifications warred with Earth traditionalism. Ringing the bell ended a round in Earth Standard, but Kalendris colony used two different bells to mark points in a scored bout, with each fighter getting audio confirmation of a clean strike. Slipping a punch was a dodge in most forms but an illegal technique in Orionese Line Boxing.

If Vice Admiral Quatermain had been a local devotee, he might have kept up with the supreme general. But if anything, he only confused Eric further with an incomplete understanding based on an older sister who wrote sports romances. Coincidentally, Eric had a copy of *The Old One-Two* in the Grand Village Library, free to replicate in any world that needed it, but the details on the boxing weren't even consistent within the pages. Though the relationship between Tracy Tatum and Sam Steubin seemed more about sweat and sculpted muscle than athletic jargon.

"I don't care if we have to run the next whole goddamn administration from down here," General Bob continued. "We need our people on the outside to get off their asses and track down every last conspirator. Every supplier who didn't triple-check credentials. Every security checkpoint that glanced instead of scanning. Every landlord who might have given a hardcoin discount to keep a lease off the omni. I want these poisonous weeds pulled up by the roots before any of us sets foot outside again. They got inside our security perimeter once, and I want to be damn sure they're not still lurking. One clean load of plasma through the right skull, and we're in chaos at the worst possible time.

"In parallel, I want psyops working on our target admirals. The imperial loyalists might not join *us*, but if we can convince a few to fracture off and drop out of Earth's pocket, we can worry about them later. Also, I think it's time to bring fleet action to the core. No... to Sol! If we can seize control of the Great Moons, we can leave Earth isolated in the solar core."

How many more moons did General Bob want? Eric wondered. Phobos and Deimos were givens. They had Ganymede locked up. Titan was practically a planet and firmly on Earth's side. And it wasn't like Europa, Io, or Callisto were liable to change sides without a LOT of fighting.

But that was Stooie Quatermain's assessment, not Eric's. Eric had no idea how any of this all worked. It was too many people. Too many ideas. Reducing populations in the hundreds of millions or small billions to mere names on a galactic map was an abstraction too far.

All of it was too much.

But he couldn't just sneak away.

Well, he probably *could* find a way to magic and lie and disguise and wheedle his way to freedom. It would involve several new applicants to the Villain Intervention Project, but he felt like it was doable.

What Eric *couldn't* abide was letting these crazy, militaristic Martians throw whole planets into chaos and kill millions to adjust the squiggles on a few maps.

He could put a stop to this.

Murder would only move the problem. The opportunity to kill 94 top officials and slink away to spend years cleaning the stain from his conscience had passed. Fewer than a quarter of the relevant parties had made it to this underground stronghold, and Eric wasn't even prepared to slaughter the ones he had in front of him.

He needed a *real* solution.

What if he found a way to turn back time? Sure, everyone had told him it wasn't possible, but so much of what he did fell under that ratty, hole-riddled umbrella that he couldn't take the claims at face value. His own failures to do any better than create a loop, which he hadn't started prior to the origins of this mess, couldn't be the final word on the matter.

What if...?

What... if... ?

What if time really *was* a loop? A big loop. An *entire* loop. Beginning to end. Wrapping around. Starting over.

Big bang.

Space rocks.

Dinosaurs.

Monkeys.

Babylonians.

Scientists.

Lunchtime Letters.

Same universe. Same people. Like a holovid rerun, happening just like before every time around.

If Eric could go forward far enough, he'd start the loop again. His time loop to save Dad might have been the clue that the universe thought in loops.

It wouldn't be easy. He'd have doubted it was the right solution if it was. But if Eric could launch himself so far forward in time that he came out the back end, he could change a near-identical universe with him as the only variable.

But where to make a change so momentous?

People claimed that the Earth/Mars fracture wasn't Eric's fault. But maybe this *wasn't* his first time through the loop. Maybe he already ruined one timeline and failed to remember it. It wouldn't be the first time he'd intentionally forgotten something.

And what parts of his current life would he lose?

Reconnecting with Jessie?

Getting to go on a grand adventure with Trebla?

Ever meeting Charlotte in the first place?

Eric had been steeling himself against personal hardships with the first two. But the possibility of never getting to know Charlotte—whether at Oxford or after the pirate rescue—hit him in the gut so hard that the admirals to either side of Stooie Quatermain gave a quick glance before deciding he wasn't worth checking on.

No.

Eric would figure something out. But he wasn't going to sacrifice his happiness in the process. He didn't need a solution right this second. He just needed to survive and, ideally, keep Mars from causing galactic calamity. In the meantime, he'd work it all out.

If it took until Plan ZXQ—or longer!—he was going to have his cake, eat it too, and share it with everyone he cared about.

After all, he had all the time in the galaxy.

▭

The fact that Earth hadn't made any provisions for getting their shuttle back strongly implied that they'd installed some kind of tracking device. As she landed it in the *Arete's* hangar, Jessie still hadn't decided whether any amount of scanning and disassembly could convince her it was clean and safe to keep long term.

They touched down with a little thud.

"Not bad," Carl commented from the copilot's seat. "Command hasn't made you *too* rusty."

Jessie kept her grumbles inward. He'd noticed. Of *course* he had. Since taking kip-tie-mahl lessons, she'd noticed a little clumsiness when it came to tech. She'd clear a pilot's cert no problem, even probably qualify as a starfighter pilot if she re-enlisted. But she wouldn't have been top of her class anymore.

But Jessie *wasn't* a starfighter pilot anymore. She wasn't special operations for Earth Navy. The *Arete* was her ship. Everyone in the hangar waiting to shower them with welcome was *her* crew. She didn't need to be able to fly circles around eyndar pilots or dogfight colonial militia. If anyone cared to bring up her shortcomings, she could flying-spin-kick them through a bulkhead.

With a glance at her smirking father as she unbuckled from the pilot's seat, she considered doing just that to him.

Comm silence had seemed only prudent on the way here. The *Arete* could lurk in Earth territory, in the vast hidden cracks between planets and notable stars, and only be at minimal risk if discovered. The rendezvous plan had been intended to shorten the peril to the escapees, if any, from the rescue mission.

Days without contact, with only Dad for company, had been...

Well, it had bothered her not knowing the status of her ship and crew, but her father's company had been remarkably less than horrible.

"Hey, hey, hey!" Carl announced, arms wide, as the boarding ramp dropped to allow them off.

Then again, he'd always been kind of fine when it was just the two of them. He was at his most obnoxious in front of an audience, whether it was Mom, Eric, and Ozzy or a couple dozen drunks at a knockoff British pub.

A round of applause broke out from the gathering in the hangar awaiting the returning heroes. Didn't those idiots know they were just feeding an addiction? And didn't they realize that it was her and Mort that had done all the work? Aunt Tiffany had basically crammed the two of them into this shuttle with Dad in a bathrobe and slippers, reeking of expensive beer and scented bath oils.

Carl took a bow, clutching a rolled-up baton of a canvas in his hand, the same canvas she'd been forbidden to touch lest Jessie ruin its resale value. Now, the priceless masterpiece (she presumed) waved like a royal scepter as her father accepted the adulation of her crew.

As the cheers died down, Jessie emerged, and the crew roared. Self-conscious, she flashed a tight smile and a quick salute before Charlotte swooped in to rescue her.

"Captain, welcome home," her XO called out, sounding weird and looking weirder. She'd heard her own voice often enough in recordings to know it, but it was supposed to be limited to playback of things she'd actually said, not new words coming out of a life-sized, fully tangible doppelganger.

"Status report?" Jessie inquired, unprepared for the hug that came instead of a list of how her command had fared in her absence.

Powerful arms clamped around her. "We're alright, here. The *Arete* is on course to meet up with the *Scylla*."

That rang a tiny alarm bell in her brain. "Shouldn't you have already picked up Eric by now?"

"They don't have him," Charlotte replied in Jessie's whispered voice. "We're meeting up to transfer personnel and take over the lead in the pickup operation."

Now the hug made sense. Jessie nonetheless extracted herself from it. She kept her voice down as Charlotte fell in beside her. Carl had the rest of the crew distracted, regaling them with tales of his misadventure, framed as an Odysseus-like journey in which he was a noble hero rather than a dumbass who'd run off to find his vigilante sister and gotten captured. "Where is he?"

"Unknown. The team from Earth was wiped out, and the leaked intel about the failed attack on the Martian nominating convention accounts for everyone *but* him. Sparta has reassured me that had he perished, she should have felt the ripple— whatever that means. I don't pretend to understand oracles, but I *do* know your brother better than anyone. I fear he's gotten himself stuck somewhere on Mars and doesn't know how to extricate himself in any satisfactory manner."

Jessie hadn't found a word to wedge into that monologue until Charlotte paused for breath. "We went comm dark. What's the political fallout? Any word from Mort's end?"

Charlotte harrumphed daintily, which sounded weird. Jessie resolved never to use her own vocal cords for that. "Mordecai has slaughtered most of the imperial loyalists at the top of the government. He's largely being hailed as some biblical angel of vengeance. Mostly, in my opinion, because the ones who'd loudly hold a contrary opinion are still smoldering. He *was* emperor, let's not forget. He knew who propped him up, and he seems to have expertly undercut his own foundations."

There were times, growing up, when Jessie had wondered whether she had a guardian angel looking out for her. Mom had tried too hard to keep her on a short leash. Dad had let her run free. The gap between evading Mom's swaddling safety and the point at which Dad had showed up at a decommissioned mid-core sewage bypass to drag her home from an unsanctioned Bronze League fight had been considerable.

She'd known how to take care of herself. Dates that didn't end well knew better than to come looking for her at the ship.

But Eric?

He wandered off as much as Jessie and with little sense

between his ears. Sure, maybe he didn't openly go looking for beatable gambling games, a quick high, or to fool around as a teenager. But he hadn't been much of a wizard back then, either.

Maybe *he* was the one with the guardian angel looking out for him. How many times had Uncle Enzio brought Eric home after a prolonged wander worried everyone? It had become a joke. Ha. Ha. Silly Eric. Got lost again. Took a wizard to find him.

In retrospect, Jessie had to wonder how many murders Eric had witnessed as a kid.

"Eric will be fine," Jessie assured Charlotte as they reached the lift. Much as she wouldn't mind a shower, a beer, and a fresh uniform, she felt a duty to check in on the bridge first. "He's far from helpless."

"I'm more worried he's embroiled himself in somehow fixing whatever troubles he may have caused."

That did sound like the sort of self-imposed bullshit Eric might pull. Jessie didn't want to dwell on that. Last thing she needed right now was to get furious at her brother for making things hard on everyone around him. "Well, be thankful for the delay. Wouldn't be much of a homecoming with two of me and none of you here."

Charlotte sneered. "Your taste in undergarments alone was enough to make me eager for a return to my own form."

Suddenly suspicious, Jessie checked out her own duplicated body. "What am I wearing under that uniform?"

"I kept up the ruse with the shapeless burlap you insisted upon. But once the need for impersonation passed, I raided my own dresser for silk panties. And, as one might have mentioned to you at some point, you do not, in the strictest fashion sense, require a bra."

Face flushing, Jessie looked away, somehow embarrassed in both the first and second person.

The two women stood shoulder to shoulder, facing the lift doors as their ride ended.

"You can't be back to normal soon enough."

"Agreed. And if you feel a need for reciprocity, I assure you that spending weeks in my own body would come with far more comfortable attire. And less perspiration."

▭

He'd forgotten how good the food had been around here. Not that the cooking aboard the *Arete* had been bad, but on Earth, Mort had kept the galaxy's top chefs at his beck and call. Now, once more floating in that orbit, even the snacks at a catered backroom political meeting delighted the tastebuds.

Ellie LeMont peered through science goggles at a datapad. "Orion is promising its delegation will be departing for Earth tomorrow."

Mort chewed possibly the best churro of his life as he nodded. "Fine. As long as they're all from the approved list. Anyone else tries to take a senatorial oath, burn them on the spot."

Brian Four Eagles cleared his throat. "You mean, *you'll* burn them on the spot?" The interim Minister of Shit Mort Didn't Want to Deal With lacked subtlety at times, but this was a deft ploy to get an answer from the guy in charge.

"Nah. Me hanging around too long wouldn't be good. Suns don't set like they used to, and I'm not much for riding horses, so come up with your own analogy. But I need to make myself scarce before people start thinking *why not just let* him *keep the job?*"

Gasps and grumbles greeted that pronouncement. As if these chicken-footed sycophants couldn't read between the tea leaves. Mort had been dropping hints as soon as he finished dropping bodies that this wasn't his gig. You get a pest problem, the exterminator comes and deals with it. No one expects the fellow to take over as landlord once the rats and insects are dead.

"But... the senate hasn't even reconvened. It's a whole new system. Someone's going to have to guide Earth through the period of turmoil," Ellie protested.

"Look," Mort stated firmly. "It's not a hard system. They had it on Earth in a million little countries. One big senate is a mess. Two little ones is better. A House of Magic. A House of Science. Science has elections. Magic appoints apprentices as successors. One gets you stability; the other, representation."

"But that's the *goal*. We're not there yet," Lawrence Lessig chimed in. "We have an idea for a new democratic Earth. Leaving the process rudderless will result in chaos that will only serve to undermine the new government."

Lessig was a professor of ancient law at Harvard, a face with vaguely familiar features seen on campus here and there where wizardly and mundane academic types crossed paths. Apparently, people respected the shit out of this guy. Possibly because he had a vague wizardly look about him.

"It won't be rudderless. It just won't be my hand on the till." Mort could appreciate a scientist leaning into an analogy Mort could roll with. "I'm going to be taking my leave of Earth. Quietly. No press. No farewell banquet. Just a chauffeur and a little shuttle, and a travel vector off Earth with no questions asked." He dearly hoped he'd used the term properly, since *vector off planet* X was Carl-speak for permission to depart someplace. "From that shuttle, I'll place a comm that will take care of everything."

Tiffany Bell reclined across the seat of a booth meant for six people, partially encircling a round table in a raised section of Club Électrique. Her feet propped on a duffel bag that, for the moment, contained exactly zero human remains.

Low purplish floodlamps and primitive laser effects lit an overhead fog pumped in through the vents. Soulless digital music thudded through the floors and furniture. Nearby, a gyrating assortment of youths overflowed a designated dance floor.

A server came around, deftly cutting through the chaos, to deliver a pitcher of beer and four glasses to Tiffany's booth.

"Just me," she apologized, flashing Convo credit. "You can take back the glasses." When the server made to depart with three of the pint-sized drinking vessels, Tiffany clarified, "All four." Then, she hoisted the pitcher to make her point.

The cold suds slid down in gulps.

She closed her eyes and savored.

"Mind if I join you?" a slick, smooth voice inquired.

"Yes." She didn't even look.

Tonight wasn't a fishing trip for someone to manually relax her. She'd charge the Convocation for a cheap massage someplace shady if the beer didn't get the job done on its own.

Halfway through the pitcher, her pocket chimed the opening bars of *Massacre Skirt*. Few modern songs spoke to the soul, but Tiffany had seriously considered a red leather miniskirt for a variety of practical, job-related reasons, thanks to Gwenda Laken. After listening to the snippet twice fully through, Tiffany fished the pestering device out of her pocket.

It wasn't *supposed* to make noise at all. Someone had turned that "feature" off for her. That meant that either the tech was on the fritz or—

"Shit."

—someone with tech-savvy helpers and a willingness to risk pissing her off was comming her from Earth.

The identifier read simply: BPP.

It had been her own shorthand. The letters stood for Boston Prime Palace. Khosrau used to ping her from that ID when he was still being piloted by Mort. There weren't a ton of people who had access to that ID, fewer who'd dare put themselves on a direct line to the librarian with the highest kill count of the present decade.

"Who is this?" she snapped upon hitting Accept. "I'm on sabbatical."

"*Sabbatical? Sure,*" Hadrian replied. But despite recognizing the voice, she was going to have to get used to thinking of it as belonging to Mordecai The Brown, now. "*You can have one after you do a teensy favor.*"

"I don't owe you jack shit. In fact, I should really start coming up with ways *you* can pay *me* back for bailing your sorry ass out of that mess."

"*You didn't want to test me, and I'd have regretted having to kill you.*"

The lava-blooded devil probably even believed that. By the time Jessie caught up with her after springing her father from his gilded cage, the fighting had been over. Hell, she'd barely had time to drag the spoiled prisoner out the door when the kid had showed up. Even if Mort had the guts to hold her magic at a standstill, could Jessie have done the dirty work?

A question Tiffany might lose sleep over, if she ever truly slept.

"Whatever you need, the answer is 'no.'"

"*The favor isn't for me. I've already left Earth, in fact.*"

Tiffany chugged from her pitcher. "Good for you. Did enough damage on your way out, though, huh?"

"*You've seen the newsfeeds?*"

"Yeah. Call it morbid curiosity."

"*What do you think of the new arrangement?*"

"Makes sense. Better than the shitty old system. They were just begging for a wizard coup, when you look back at it. But you know me. I'm not political."

"*You'll pick it up as you go.*"

Tiffany nearly choked on her beer. "Mort... what did you do?"

"*I made them promise to hold the press release off for a couple hours, but you're going to be announced as Dictator of Earth, overseer of getting the new constitutional republic off the ground.*"

"YOU FUCKING MAXIMUSED ME?" she shouted at the device loudly enough for dancers to check on the commotion. Self-conscious now, she took her feet down, sat up in the booth, and set aside the pitcher. "You can't be fucking serious. I'm qualified for *one* job, and I've already got it."

"*You're the perfect choice. You're powerful enough personally and have a dark enough reputation that no one is liable to question your authority.*"

"Authority I've got no business with. If you want Earth fucked up, you couldn't pick someone better to botch the job."

"*The politicians know the drill. You just keep anyone from stopping the orderly march back from imperial rule. The rest is entirely up to your judgment.*"

Tiffany fumed. "And if I decide that we can only have stability if the entire harem is executed, along with any imperial heirs?"

"*I don't think you would, but I'm giving up oversight, so it's not my call.*" She was wrong. Mort didn't have molten rock in his veins, just straight ice. "*But I'd recommend talking that stuff over with your new advisers. In a couple hours, they'll either be advising you or vilifying you on every galactic newsfeed for shirking your duty to Earth."*

"I hate you."

"You hate everyone, and me less than most."

"You SO owe me for this."

"You know, you young people... Give them unchecked power over a sizable galactic empire, and they can't think of a way to make that work out for them..."

The comm ended.

Tiffany drained the last of her beer and headed for the exit, pondering.

Just what *could* she get out of this? Maybe a retirement moon? A castle?

Maybe this wouldn't be the worst career move. Plus, she could probably work pro bono for the library once she'd taken her reward.

But still, fuck Mort.

Harmony studied the scans. The glossy black background of her datapad reflected the goggles she wore with an entirely different set of results. Years of practice had left her able to process the information in moderate detail simultaneously, which was fine for simple cases. And her current patient was, at present, a simple case.

If only the rest of him were so easy to deal with.

"So, will I live?" Carl inquired brightly.

Pretending to ignore him, Harmony opened a voice recording file. "Subject is a 64-year-old male. Height, 177 cm. Weight, 99.8kg."

"Ooh, I kept it under a hundred. Lemme take a piss though. I think we can knock half a kilo off that."

"Heart and liver show normal function. Liver slightly overworked. Hormone levels worryingly high."

"How worryingly...?"

Harmony continued as if he hadn't said anything. "Visual acuity excellent despite advanced age."

"Yeah, go back to that hormone thing..."

"Mild hearing loss."

"You're overlooking the red flag you just threw."

"No detectable signs of brain activity."

"Hey! That's slander! I—wait a minute."

Harmony shot him a smirk. "You're fine. Better than you have any right to be after your ordeal. Those imperial doctors took care of whatever the eyndar did to you well enough that I can hardly detect it. As far as the hormones, I suspect your poor wife has been dealing with that as long as you've known her. I am, however, going to recommend a bloodstream and digestive flush."

"Sounds... unpleasant. Is there any way we could *not* do that?"

"It's all H-tech drones. A quick injection, which you'll hardly feel, followed a few hours from now by some discoloration of your stool. You'll feel years younger."

"Really?"

Harmony sighed from her toes. Sometimes that damned Hippocratic Oath was an absolute albatross around her neck. "Yes. Really. A year from now, that kind of treatment will probably run you a hundred thousand terras. You're welcome."

When faced with no outright objections, Harmony administered the pneumatic injection with a hand tool Trebla had put together that fit both doctor and patient anatomy better than the haathee version she'd found upon taking over as chief medical officer.

"Can you answer a question for me about these drones?"

Carl asked, rubbing the shoulder where she'd injected those very drones just a few heartbeats earlier.

"Before would have been a better time to ask. But, of course."

"Can they be transmitted sexually?"

"No."

"What if I tried really hard? I don't plan on dragging Amy out here, and I doubt you make house calls, so if you just maybe, top me up a little, I can—"

"Out," Harmony ordered. She hit a comm panel on the wall. "Captain, your father is fine. I'm discharging him, effective immediately. He's not my problem anymore."

"Copy that. Hope he wasn't too big a pain in the ass."

"The usual."

"Sorry about that."

Harmony ended the comm.

Carl slid off the examination table and straightened his shirt. "Okie, dokie, Doc. Don't need to tell *me* where I'm not wanted."

Harmony scowled. "No one has time for a list that size."

As soon as Carl was gone from Med Bay, however, a weight lifted from Harmony's shoulders.

It was more than being free of one annoying patient. He'd been a mission. Actually, he'd been responsible for several of the *Arete's* recent diversions from helping the galaxy at large. With his nonsense dealt with, the rest of them could get back to making life easier, safer, and healthier for the Milky Way's residents.

Earth was on a path back to sane government. Mars couldn't hold onto their dictatorial ways without Earth as a villain. The galaxy was shaping up.

Heading back to her office, Harmony opened a private text comm on her goggles.

Got a minute? Come see me.

Britney appeared within seconds. "What's up, Doc?"

Harmony got up from her desk and went to the wall. She triggered the concealed drawer. "I just wanted you here for this."

The incubation chamber was in standby mode. She'd started and stopped the process so many times by now, she couldn't imagine how actual pregnant women went through an entire natural gestation without losing their minds. But now it felt right. She had time. She had the mental focus to devote to a newborn.

She had a while left to wait, even on accelerated incubation.

Harmony triggered the sequence.

"Going through with it?" Britney asked from right behind her.

"I was always going to."

"How long?"

"I've left the machine some leeway in making that determination. I... I wanted at least a little sense of surprise and wonder."

"Hours, days, weeks...?"

"A week or two. Approximately. I'll get an alert with an hour or two remaining."

Two huge, soft, solid arms enveloped Harmony, wrapping her like a safety harness. Britney's whole body was a warm, reassuring wall behind her. "Thank you."

Harmony smiled. "I didn't do anything. I just wanted someone with me to share this moment."

"Thank you for choosing me as that someone."

Harmony's heartbeat quickened. They'd discussed life after the *Arete*. Britney wanted to be a part of the H-tech revolution, and Harmony trusted her to remain at her side.

After all, Britney had been willing to risk her life on this crazy ride when it was only about helping people. No megacorp profits. No lavish rewards. Just the simple joys of curing and healing those in need.

Britney was liable to know the baby for a long time. To be part of her life. It had seemed only natural to invite her.

"Have you picked a name yet?"

"Not yet."

"Can I put in a vote for 'Britney Jr.'?"

Harmony laughed. "That would just get confusing."

Britney turned her around. Their eyes met through panes of multi-layer data display. Britney pushed up Harmony's goggles. Her own eyes were so bright with hope.

━━━

From one side of the hookah, a ring of smoke floated, expertly formed, away from the mouth of an experienced imbiber. On the other, a living fire hose sprayed the room with a swirling, abstract artwork of fog.

Grosstet had set up a spare holo-projector in the hookah lounge, and he and Figgy had been watching human newsfeeds for hours.

"THEY HAVE DONE THIS BEFORE, YES?"

"It's a variant on a government they used on and off for centuries before unifying under a single planetary government."

The haathee commodore sucked another breath of the smoke, gurgling the filtration water in the central receptacle. "SO THEY KNOW IT DOES NOT WORK?"

Figgy snickered languidly. "You'd be *amazed* what humans can not know. They know it's a bad idea to fuck coworkers. You think they don't do that?"

Grosstet had been around the *Arete* long enough to know otherwise for certain.

"They try to get rich gambling. Does that work?"

Grosstet could draw on personal experience with poker to know better.

"They know you don't get anywhere in life smoking *this* stuff." Figgy waggled the mouthpiece of his end of the hookah for emphasis. "WE ARE NOT HUMAN. NONE OF THEM ARE HERE."

"I'm here more often than most." Grosstet knew this to be a massive understatement. "Trust me, plenty of humans enjoy a good smoke, too. And as a species, they don't learn jack shit."

"THEY HAVE MANY SCIENTISTS."

"Science, schmience." This was a less compelling counterargument than the haathee was willing to accept, but he chose not to object outright. "They come up with new *facts* all the time. But the core, the real meat and bananas of living? You can read ancient human poems, shit that got passed by word of mouth for centuries before someone thought to jab a stick into some clay and make a written language, and it's the same shit, different century.

"Guy can't keep it in his pants, gets murdered by an angry husband. King fights a war over a stretch of land his neighbor's got, dies in battle. Treat your kid like shit to toughen him up for the 'real world,' then find out the 'real world' doesn't include taking in elderly parents when they get sick. Raise the price on Tabaxinol by 2cT a dose, some upstart company decides to develop an alternative and you lose 94 percent of your market share inside a year."

The latter was topical, since the tribulations of Aerith Medical Group had been playing out across the text scrawl below more pressing galactic news.

"WHY NOT STUDY HISTORY IF THE OUTCOMES ARE SO OBVIOUS?"

"Those who don't study history just repeat it. Which usually sucks. Those that *do* study history end up tearing their fur out by the handful watching imbeciles fuck up the galaxy they all share. It's a no-win. I can respect the decision for ignorance as an alternative to hashish for dealing with the inevitable."

"I CAN CHANGE THE GALAXY. SHOULD I NOT SMOKE THIS?"

Figgy took a long drag. "Sir, you are a grown-ass elephant four times my age. I can enlighten you on the local culture and my personal beliefs, but in no galaxy have I got any business telling you what you should or shouldn't do."

Grosstet paused. The laaku made sense, which was never a good sign. He was a delightful jester filled with nonsensical pseudo-wisdom and amusing anecdotes. A worthy companion for relaxation, but no kind of adviser.

Was Grosstet's brain suffering from the smoke? He took stock. No. His thoughts were very thinkful, and his brain was braining brainishly.

He stopped himself.

"BRAINISHLY. A HUMAN WORD OR NOT?"

"Not."

The haathee shook his head. Maybe brainishly wasn't a word, but his brain was knocking on the inside of his skull, and Grosstet finally got the message. "PERHAPS I HAVE BEEN TOO LONG WITHOUT THE COMPANY OF MY OWN KIND."

━━

Two days after Carl's return to the *Arete*, and it was like he'd never left. As Jessie read the daily departmental reports, each section of the ship seemed to have one or two complaints about him.

Misappropriation of materials.

Bothering subordinates.

Inflicting live music on the Soundcheck Saloon's patrons.

Encouraging insubordination in others.

Gambling operations.

Unauthorized removal of alcoholic beverages from common stores.

Obstructing Logistics' efforts to reassign furnishings.

Inappropriate behavior in Med Bay.

Charlotte had run a tight ship as Jessie. The real Jessie had to wonder whether she'd have been able to pull off that same level of efficiency and orderliness with Carl Ramsey aboard.

But among all the petty annoyances, there were bright spots, too.

Chief among these was a comm from her Aunt Jamie.

Jessie had Daphne patch it through the bridge holo-comm system. Aunt Jamie's face appeared, triple life-sized. "Want me to grab my father?"

Jamie Ramsey shook her head emphatically. "Nope. I'm meeting that little bastard face-to-face, not over a comm. I've avoided it this long, I'm seeing Brad in person."

"He *really* doesn't go by Brad anymore," Jessie warned.

"He'll get over it. Look, I was just contacting you to let you know we'll be a few hours late to the rendezvous."

"Cold feet?"

"Cold starship. Picked up an odd distress call and an odder passenger. Now I need to ditch some amnesiac Convocation liaison pilot and scrub his computer logs before I head for the agreed coordinates."

"Liaison?" Jessie echoed. "Who'd be out there getting chauffeured around by...?" Recent newsfeeds echoed in her ears. Aunt Tiffany had been given full control over the democratic transition process. Ministers and Grand Councilors had held press conferences. "You've got Mort aboard, don't you."

"Says he's Mordecai The Brown. Matches the wizard who let himself show up on the feeds in Geneva Prime. But I met Mordecai The Brown, a million years back, and he should be a shriveled prune of an old fuck by now."

"I believe him. It's a long story, and he'll probably tell it himself if you offer a few beers. But on the off chance that it's an elaborate ruse, the guy just murdered hundreds of senators and Boston Prime's most loyal imperialist wizards, not to mention Khosrau the First-and-Hopefully-Only. If he wants to say he's Mordecai The Brown, Merlin himself, or a potted cactus named Larry, I'm just going to fucking roll with it."

"Copy that. Story or no story, guy's got unlimited beer privileges while he's here. Whoever he is, he saved Brad's ass. Oh, and you too, I gather."

"I was also there," Jessie added. She wasn't sure how she felt about her involvement. She'd been more than a traveling companion, less than an equal partner. If she hadn't been there using her body as a sledgehammer to shatter the limbs, heads, and torsos of Mort's adversaries, maybe he could have pulled off the coup anyway. Maybe if Aunt Tiffany or Wizard Lemonface von Pointybeard had stuck around, maybe she'd have been the ace up Mort's sleeve to win anyway. Or maybe him having an old-fashioned fist-based murder machine along was the warning one or both needed to opt against valor.

Then again, once Mort took credit publicly for the carnage, Jessie's role had been swept under the nearest rug instantly. It was nice to hear someone at least acknowledge she'd played a role.

"Well, I'm not forgetting. I've got what, like twenty-four birthdays to make up for? I'll add it to the list."

"Twenty-nine, I think," Jessie replied with a smirk. "Not sure about the etiquette of time-traveler birthdays. My expert on the subject is still MIA."

"Don't worry. My people on Mars still haven't heard anything, and I think General Bob and his cronies would make noise about it if they captured or killed a wizard with Eric's profile."

Great. As if Jessie didn't already dread the newsfeeds enough these days. Now she had to brace herself for news of Eric's death being boasted about on MNN. Just thinking about it boiled her blood.

"Tell you what. If that's what happens, I'm parking the *Arete* in high Martian orbit and turning the planet into a donut with New Vancouver as the hole."

"Do you... like actually...?"

"As far as I know? Maybe. Grosstet's never said what our theoretical maximum firepower is in any terms I can wrap my head around."

"Well, just keep in mind that a few billion Martians will have had nothing to do with it and probably don't deserve antimatter annihilation."

"You're sucking the fun out of my vengeance fantasy."

"Trust me. You don't want dreams like that healthy and thriving in your psyche. Maybe talk it over with that counselor of yours."

"She's stuck looking and sounding just like me. Probably do my brain more harm than good. Once you get Mort back here to change her back... well... she'll probably be on my side about avenging Eric."

Aunt Jamie had a knowing smirk that looked just like Dad's. "Tell ya what... You people are a mess over there."

"Sorry."

"Nah. Means you're doing things right. If being a Samaritan vigilante ever turns into punch-clock office work, that's when you know you've lost your orbit. My helmswoman just updated our course. Transmitting our ETA presently. Ramsey out."

"Ramsey out," Jessie echoed just in time for the comm to cut short.

Mindy leaned over from the Tactical station. "So's ya know, you try threading Mars like a necklace bead, I don't care what sort of magic laaku kung fu you done learnt, I'm puttin' you on yer arse."

Without looking back, Jessie kept her voice low. "You'd better."

━━

Jamie fretted at her seat, struggling to twirl spaghetti around her fork without it slipping off repeatedly. The menu selection had been picked by their guest, and he seemed unconcerned about the discomfiture he caused the other diners at the captain's private mess.

Not that her quarters were anything fancy. They had to tip the bed up to make room for the table, after all.

The five of them crowded around the rectangular table. Jamie and Sofia took the heads at either end, still close enough that they could reach across and hold hands. Dr. Zazel and Kinniss shared one long side. Opposite them, the young man with the old soul had one whole side to himself, and he was having no trouble at all spooling up his pasta.

Mordecai The Brown—or whoever he really was—wagged

one tight-wound bundle of noodles as he held court. "You know, it's the oregano. Most places these days take too light a hand with it. Might as well be dousing your spaghetti in ketchup for all the complexity it's got. Basil most sauciers know how to use. But whoever you've got cooking clearly knows Earth classical cuisine."

Kinniss snickered. "She's plouph."

The guest list for the private soiree had been selected with English skills in mind. But that was naive on Jamie's part on two fronts. First off, the guy spoke better eyndar than most of her crew. Second, after a few brief conversations, she'd determined that she wasn't qualified to argue with him in their shared native tongue. Instead, Mordecai jumped between languages with fluid ease.

He answered Kinniss's comment in Jiara. "Well, pass along my compliments. Far be it from me to claim my own species does its cuisine best." How the hell the guy had picked up on the fact that Kinniss had grown up in a largely azrin refugee camp and spoke their language best eluded Jamie. Maybe he had a hitch somewhere in his accent or grammar. The guy certainly didn't go around background checking himself to people; he was her fucking security chief, after all.

"You miss human food?" Sofia inquired. "I know I do sometimes. We don't go a la carte often, and the majority pick isn't often Earth food."

"Miss it? I've hardly gotten away from it. I've talked our tesud cook around on the idea of clam chowder, and the campus dining hall at Oxford deserves a Silde engine in my book, even if they're a little too menu-heavy toward the subcontinent for my preference. But the *Arete* isn't big on proper Earth food. They've got one of those contraptions that can make food that looks like anything, and I seem to be in the minority that finds it all comes out tasting like the wrapper real food should have come in. Hard to convince someone to toil at a stovetop when instant science sludge will splorge itself onto a plate on command."

Jamie hadn't often had the chance to sample laaku enzymatically reconstituted proteins, and Mordecai was doing an excellent job dissuading her from seeking out the experience. "Most of us have gotten pretty used to eyndar recipes. Ingredients are easier to come by in our usual hunting grounds."

Mordecai chuckled. "That how you've kept so young?"

She dropped her fork with a clatter onto her plate and switched to English. "Now I *know* you're taking the piss. I'm more spare parts than original, and if I ran on fuel rods, I'd be scraping the inside of the injection chamber for residue at this point. I don't know what fountain of youth *you* stumbled into, but—"

"Body-snatching," Mordecai replied casually. "Last couple were hijackings. This one I traded for a few thousand planets and a groveling senate. You're wondering if I'm the real McCoy. But I remember meeting you a few lifetimes back. My first. Your only. I convinced you not to turn over Chuck and Becky to Galactic Child Services in exchange for looking after them."

There had only been the two of them there. It was possible that Brad had heard about and told whoever this was. It was more likely that this murderous wizard was the genuine article. "Gotta check. When was the last time you, me, and Brad were in the same place?"

"Some shitstain planetside Earth Navy training base. Sofia was there too. Didn't get the impression you two were an item yet. It was the only time Michelle remembered you from. By the by, I know you barely knew her, and Rhi was too young to even know you enough to miss you, but you should reach out."

This was too much. Jamie's spaghetti started getting blurry, and her cybernetic implants weren't correcting for the distortion. "Right. Yeah. How the girls doing these days?"

"Michelle works at a top catering service in New Shanghai. Rhiannon inherited your grandparents' place in New Cali."

"What's she do?" For all the research she'd done keeping up with Brad's career and personal life, and the extensive research into Jessie, Jamie had largely overlooked her little sisters.

Mordecai chewed a bite of his pasta and shrugged. "She used to perform a lounge act. Had one original song that got popular a while back. Royalties keep groceries on her table, near as I can tell, without her having to work. Other than that, she smokes cheap local weed and dates a different fellow every few months."

It was like walking into a library of old paper books. A bunch of leather spines with titles, but crack one open, and there were whole worlds inside. There was one book, in particular, she couldn't wait to read.

"And... um... Brad? What's he like these days? In person, I mean. I've... I mean... I get a lot of intel... maybe kept an eye out... but what's he really like?"

Mordecai set down his silverware and pushed away his empty plate. Tipping his chair back, he took a long breath. "Where to even get started about that boy...?"

━━━

The bunker hadn't changed, really. But every day that passed, it *felt* smaller. Eric had settled into the routine that best matched how Stooie Quatermain responded to similar conditions set up for him in the Village of Eternity.

He woke up to a cheap plastic alarm clock bleating from the nightstand beside his bunk.

He took a shower.

He pretended to shave but used magic to remove this face's stubble lest he slit his own throat using traditional shaving rituals.

Breakfast was two eggs (runny) and two slices of bacon (soggy), plus a half grapefruit that he took a few nibbles from.

The rest of the day was impromptu briefings, called together with the faintest of pretense and the flimsiest of news about the investigation into the convention center attack.

Eric's co-conspirators had been killed. They'd been enchanted such that their corpses and spirits wouldn't give up evidence. What everyone topside was looking for, and failing to find, was him.

Their failure to find the lynchpin of the operation had started this whole sequestration. No one had given "Let's Hide All the Important People in an Isolated Bunker" a name, but in his head, Eric had begun calling it Operation Hidden Candy.

When you think someone's after a stash of Starberry Chews or a bag of Yoodle-Oohs you saved for later after the last planetside adventure, you don't deny it. You don't even acknowledge the sugary treat's existence. A mere glance in the direction of a hiding spot could be enough to not only give away the fact that you have it, but risk someone coming in and snarfing down all your precious snacks before you get a chance to enjoy them.

Well, all the admirals were a military flavor pack of Starberry Chews, and Eric was the even more valuable Yoodle-Oohs, except everyone thought he was just a novelty-flavored Starberry Chew. And while, in the outside world, someone was after Starberry Chews, the admirals were still operating under the assumption that any theoretical mastermind candy was still *outside* the bag.

Anyone could spot a Yoodle-Ooh among the Starberry Chews. Longer. Rectangular. Clear plastic instead of color-coded waxy paper. But Eric wore a wrapper like all the chews and kept his mouth shut in any briefing where he could get away with it.

As he departed the 1330 Briefing About One Wizard Who Had Visited New Vancouver Two Weeks Ago—which had been about as interesting and insightful as the agenda suggested —he heard footsteps trailing him in the bunker's hallways. Slightly faster. Ever closer.

"Stooie, hold up," Admiral Hershey called out.

With an increasing feel for the role he was playing, Eric didn't consult the original before stopping and turning to let the more senior admiral catch up.

"We need to talk."

"Sure, Kenny," Eric replied casually. Stooie Quatermain rarely treated either the job or his peers with reverence. He'd grown up around fleet officers. To him, admiral was just a job like any other, no more special than a data plumber or a shoe polish repairman.

The briefing had dispersed into various disparate cliques, as usual. No one else had come this way except Eric and Admiral Hershey. Nonetheless, the other admiral felt the need to drag Eric into a pantry that reeked of potatoes and coffee beans.

"You need to cut that shit out," Hershey scolded.

"What shit?" Eric asked without needing to feign ignorance.

"Every day—every *hour*—we're stuck down here, Mars projects weakness to the galaxy. When Randall says we'll stay down here as long as it takes, he can't be hearing support."

Huh? Oh. Eric hadn't even counted his muttered affirmations and little nods as participation, let alone support that might be propping up the supreme general. Stooie just blank-checked authority. There were few enough people these days that outranked him that he even deferred to competent subordinates out of habit. After all, when was the last time Captain Annabeth or Commander Bianca had been wrong about anything important?

"Sorry."

"Sorry? The fuck is wrong with you, Quatermain?" Anyone actually referring to Eric's identity by last name outside official capacity was tantamount to a parent full-naming one of their kids. Eric was in trouble here. "You think this is some kind of game we're playing? Randall's been behind a desk too long. So someone tried to kill us all. So what? Earth's been out for blood for years, now. Now, they're showing signs of weakness, and we're scared because we heard the plasma sizzle past our ear? They missed! We need to come out strong. I've got Monroe and Stephenson with me, and the marines have been itching to get out since the start."

Eric had been able to tell *that* much himself. While General Bob got his generalship as a member of Earth Marine Corps back when it was all one big unhappy, violent family, his fellow marine generals in the bunker had advocated for a quick exit from the start. Only their religious devotion to the chain of command had kept them in check this long.

Apparently, even marines had a limit to following orders.

"You need me to... what exactly?"

Suddenly, Eric's Martian vice admiral's uniform was bunched up by the collar in one of Admiral Hershey's fists. Nose to nose, he—

Well, Eric didn't get to hear what the admiral might have been about to say. The unexpectedly physical turn of the altercation had taken him off guard, and nose to nose also meant eye to eye. Hershey had probably meant to intimidate the notoriously wishy-washy Stooie Quatermain. Instead, he'd spooked a wizard with a brain full of other people.

Now, the Village of Eternity census incremented by one.

"What the FUCK is going on?!" Hershey demanded.

Eric stood before the admiral in his own form, robed and floating just off the ground, a habit he'd picked up for impressing the newbies who might need a bit of awe to convince them they weren't in the real world any longer.

The admiral still wore his uniform, right down to the medals. But the pair were no longer in a pantry.

Towering trees loomed on all sides. A lightly trampled footpath wound into the darkness in two directions.

Uriela appeared from neither of those directions before Eric could decide how to respond to the admiral's question. "Eric... I seem to recall that during your last visit, you promised we weren't getting any unexpected guests."

"Who are you?" Hershey demanded.

Eric flapped a hand to shut the admiral up a minute, not that he used any magic or compulsion to enforce the unspoken edict. "He was an accident. There was an argument. Mostly one-sided. I waffled a little too hard and he tried grabbing me and one thing led to another and—"

Uriela leaned to look past Eric. "I don't sense a tether."

The god of the Village of Eternity forced a sheepish grin. "I... uh... pulled him all the way in before I realized."

"So, what you're saying is: there's a body?"

Eric sighed and flopped onto a beanbag chair that appeared in time to catch him. "Yeah..."

"A what?" Hershey exclaimed. "Someone tell me what's going on here this instant!"

"I know time is slow out there, but you need to deal with

this immediately," Uriela warned. She'd been kept apprised of the situation below the Martian surface and hated the whole plan, top to bottom, not the least of which because Eric was risking the immortal lifeboat keeping the millennia-old residents of the Village afloat. Including herself.

"Yeah. I know. Any ideas?"

"Get back out there. Feign ignorance. As for this one..." Uriela scowled at the admiral. "Mind if I throw him in with your tutor?"

"Yeah, he and Stooie deserve one another," Eric agreed. "Don't think I'll be referencing the cheat sheet from here on out, anyway."

Eric opened his eyes before Admiral Hershey's objection escaped his phantasm's mouth.

Now, the body of that same Mars Navy admiral crumpled limp and fell at Eric's feet. He tugged the wrinkles out of Vice Admiral Quatermain's uniform.

Stepping over the body, Eric exited the pantry, took a deep breath, and broke into a run.

"HELP! SOMEONE MURDERED ADMIRAL HERSHEY! I THINK WE'VE GOT A WIZARD HERE IN THE BUNKER WITH US!"

━━

That evening, Jessie stood there, freshly showered, freshly shaved, freshly uniformed at the head of the delegation in the *Arete's* hangar. She didn't know whom she was trying to impress. Aunt Jamie was as rough-and-tumble a spacer as Jessie Ramsey had ever met. Many who took to the stars to make their living had the veneer of planetary life chipped away over time; Aunt Jamie's veneer had been eroded away by decades of cosmic dust.

And it certainly wasn't Dad she was trying to make a good impression on. He'd made it abundantly clear that his enduring image of her was that of a whiny, petulant teenager too gullible to catch on that he'd been a master criminal.

Everyone else, except for Aunt Sofia, had spent so much time around her of late that she'd have a hard time altering anyone's opinion of her.

At her side, Charlotte shifted her weight from one foot to the other. It was a habit of Jessie's when she was impatient, and with Charlotte wearing her body, she found the imitation annoying. "Cut it out."

"Habit. Apologies. I'll make a priority of unlearning it."

Trebla's voice blared over the PA system. "*Incoming. Stand back and mind the breeze.*"

There was, of course, no wind from the airlock opening. Somewhere along the line, without her aware of its origin, the joke had caught on in the Logistics department. Apparently contagious, it now afflicted Engineering.

Of course, once the shuttle from the *Scylla* entered, she saw Trebla's point. Aunt Jamie's shuttle popped up through the hole in the hangar floor and whipped around. While it was clear enough of the welcome brigade not to hit anyone directly with ion wash, the wash itself kicked up a wake of displaced air that blew Jessie's hair back.

She still wasn't used to having hair long enough for that to happen.

From there, the shuttle settled right in for a proper, textbook landing. The ramp opened without delay.

Out of the corner of her eye, Jessie watched her father's reaction. She didn't know what to expect to see there. A grin? One of those stupid, cocksure smirks? Wonderment?

It sure as hell wasn't glassy eyes and a nervous gulp.

When the ramp finished coming down, Aunt Jamie was

standing there with Aunt Sofia a respectful step behind. For a moment, nobody moved. Then, Jamie took a timid march down toward the *Arete's* hangar. All the bluster and bravado Jessie's aunt usually brought with her, whether impersonating Jessie or as herself, was utterly absent.

A tentative smile.

A hesitant pause once both boots hit haathee steel.

Dad took a shuddering breath, not blinking, as if, were his eyes to close, she might be gone by the time they reopened.

The next step Aunt Jamie took might as well have been a starter's pistol.

Dad hadn't run so much as a kilometer over the course of Jessie's entire childhood. Now, he sprinted to meet his long-lost sister.

Jamie started on course to meet him halfway but soon switched to bracing herself as a crushing hug bowled into her. Dad bawled his eyes out.

Carl Ramsey got somber at funerals. He laughed and joked at weddings. He'd boasted at the births of his children, to hear Mom tell the tale. Jessie had never seen him like this.

No one moved to intrude on this moment.

"Tears aged like wine," Charlotte remarked softly, for Jessie's ears alone. "A vintage that predates us both."

They were older than that by far, Jessie reckoned. Dad had been a kid when Aunt Jamie went missing, presumed dead. He'd been years from meeting Mom, far longer from marrying her. Unable to take her eyes from the overwrought spectacle before her, Jessie couldn't help but think that these were more to one another than siblings.

A gruff voice from inside the shuttle brought everyone back to reality. "*Told* you he'd be happy to see you." Mort passed the still-respectful Sofia and clomped down the ramp. As he tried to give the reunited pair a wide berth, Dad shot an angry finger his way.

"How long have you known?"

Mort harrumphed. It sounded vaguely more menacing than it used to, especially compared to Uncle Enzio's signature grunt. "I had the entirety of Earth Navy Intelligence working for me, and I didn't find out until you did."

Dad got this suspicious look on his face, which was weird as Dad never let on that he didn't believe you until he'd made up his mind you were lying.

"Come on, Fartface," Aunt Jamie told Dad with a brave smirk for someone with such wet cheeks. "Let's go find someplace private to catch up on shit."

"I mostly go by Carl these days," Dad replied lamely as his big sister towed him along in a side hug that spoiled both their walking gaits.

"Hey, Jess told me you don't like Brad anymore, so I'm being respectful of that." They shared a chuckle, and Jessie found herself wondering why she never had that kind of relationship with her siblings. She envied that closeness that over forty years of estrangement couldn't wash away.

Jessie loved her brothers. But Eric lived in a dream world she couldn't see. Ozzy had been a lawyer long before setting foot in college, following the letter of the rules often in defiance of their spirit but getting away with every damn thing Jessie had gotten nailed for.

Sensing that the tender moment had passed, Sofia came down from the shuttle as well.

However, the Ramseys weren't the only ones here for a reunion. As soon as Mort was clear of Dad and Jamie, Sparta rushed him. Unlike Jamie, Mort didn't brace himself for impact. Instead, he deftly took a half step to the side. When Sparta collided with him, arms wrapped around his neck like a scarf, he swung her around, feet sweeping a meter off the ground, and spinning with her momentum until setting her down standing atop the toes of his shoes.

Their kiss was something from a holovid.

"I knew you'd be back for me," she told him after a gasp for breath. "But damned if I didn't miss you."

"My company *is* a little hard to overlook, I'd imagine." He scooped Sparta into his arms, cradling her beneath the knees and back, held high enough to continue kissing her. Though he was no gym rat, Jessie spotted the telltale signs of balance and strain in his body that suggested he wasn't using magic to hold her up. Sparta, twig that she was, didn't seem enough of a burden that Mort wasn't willing to cart her off bodily from the hangar.

Jessie gave a silent nod of greeting as the couple passed. Debriefings could wait.

That was about the point where Mort scowled and glanced from Jessie to Charlotte and back again. "Damn kind of magic you people running around here?" He spared a finger and thumb for a quick snap, and Charlotte resumed her true form.

"Ow! Warn a person!" Charlotte griped, sounding like her proper, albeit miffed, self once again. "This uniform is like a vise."

Jessie's cheeks flushed as she saw how her uniform fit her first officer, baggy and bulging in all the wrong places suddenly.

"Well, Eric should've fixed you himself," Mort grumped before lugging his girlfriend off.

Neither Jessie nor Charlotte decided that this was the right time to inform the wizard that his apprentice hadn't managed to make his way home yet.

Back in Mort and Sparta's quarters, the fresh sheets weren't so fresh any longer, and the whimsical dusting of rose petals had made a mess. Romantic candles had been reduced to lumpy waxen puddles. Still, the evening hadn't come to a conclusion.

A slender hand slapped Mort's thigh in encouragement. "My turn."

From lying side by side, Mort didn't need any convincing to roll onto his back. He was beyond exhausted already, but like she'd claimed earlier, Sparta had missed him. After the worry he must have given her, far be it from him to deny her his every comfort.

She was gorgeous. Glistening. Glowing. Clad in nothing but jewelry he'd made for her. She sang a wordless opera co-written together.

When finally, dripping sweat from loose hair, she collapsed into the crook of his arm, she caught her breath and asked a question.

"What was it in that book, anyway?"

"Are you inquiring because you didn't have to use it... or because you did?"

"A single glance burned that azrin wizard alive."

Mort chuckled. "Azrin wizard. I'd heard about him, of course. Figures those Bostonian assholes would sacrifice him rather than a second human colleague."

"It wasn't funny at the time," Sparta assured him.

He wasn't about to argue, but just picturing the scene made him think otherwise. "How'd you get him to open it?"

"I feigned an attempt to use it against him, then fumbled in my not-so-feigned terror and dropped it. He got to it first. What would have happened if I'd been the one to look?"

"You wouldn't have been. You're not an idiot. I warned you not to."

"But if I had. Humor me."

That wasn't a scene he enjoyed envisioning, but he did as asked. "You'd have seen demonic script. 'Vaieen' is the closest you'll hear the name pronounced with a human tongue. Squid-faced xenos from back when dinosaurs roamed free."

"You've told me about that tome."

"Yeah, well, the *Tome of Bleeding Thoughts* was a complete instruction manual to their concept of magic. The good. The bad. The worse. And the really, really, *really* nasty stuff. Plus, a few safeguards so that our feeble, fleshy brains wouldn't boil over like a forgotten teakettle. Even then, it takes a stern and sturdy mind to hold it all in."

"I gathered all that. What if Wizard Yarzzi had been stern enough, sturdy enough? Surely you can't have gotten lucky with the ones you've shown it to intentionally."

"Oh, that wasn't the *Tome of Bleeding Thoughts* I left with you."

Mort felt the furrow of her brow more than saw it, pressed against his chest. "Then how did it—?"

"Not the *whole* tome, leastwise. I may have edited down a Busy Wizard's Guide version for you. Mostly the nasty stuff; none of the safeguards. Maybe four or five wizards alive could have opened that book, made eye contact with the script, and lived to complain about the penmanship."

Sparta shuddered. She remained silent a long while. The two of them eventually came to breathe in sync as they relaxed.

"Marry me," she told him. There wasn't even a twitch to sit up and look him in the eye.

Mort grinned. "So, you see yourself spending a lifetime with a guy who writes lethal demonic fan fiction?"

"No. Athena high on Olympus, no! And that's the life I want. I walk around suppressing premonitions of mundane toils of my neighbors and colleagues. I want mystery. I want surprises. I want *passion*. I want *you*, Mordecai The Brown. I want to be your wife; I want to raise children with you. I want to grow frightfully old and maybe start another life or a dozen with you. I want to marry you and not leave these quarters until I'm pregnant."

Just as Mort was about to point out several logical flaws in her demands, a thin finger came to rest across his lips.

"I know. We ought to have a ceremony. Probably with our clothes on. And you'll want your best man back aboard."

"My best man's already here," Mort replied. What did she know about Eric? Was Charlotte still looking like Jessie due to his failure to return on schedule? Sweet of her to think it would be Eric at any rate, but he'd been a nephew—almost a son—but never a friend as such.

"So we'll hold off a little on making it official. We can still make good on my other condition."

Mort groaned. "My turn again, I believe?"

Sparta thwarted his efforts to get off his back. "I think we're done with your turns for a while. However, you never gave me an answer."

"Technically, you didn't ask a question."

"Since when do you take orders?"

Mort grinned up at her as Sparta settled in astride him once more. "Whenever I like."

———

This tribunal felt biased.

Eric sat on one side of a table. Across from him, the three admirals conducting the interrogation could easily have been witnesses or suspects themselves.

Once in a while, when adopting a disguise, it was an annoyance to suppress his nervous habits and portray someone else's. But Stooie Quatermain tended toward fidgeting under scrutiny, which wasn't any trouble at all to mimic. Beneath the table, Eric wrung his hands.

General Bob held court. Admirals Welker and DiBiase flanked him like the second- and third-place winners expecting to receive medals. All wore stern, unreadable expressions.

"Admiral Quatermain, you were the last one to speak with Kent Hershey before his body was discovered."

"I discovered the body," Eric interjected. "I can't be the one who killed him."

Well, lies right off the bat, then. He hadn't sat down at this table with a solid plan. Now, with an audience of basically everyone in the bunker who wasn't here as hired help, he'd opted for the Dad Method.

It was Admiral Welker who delivered the immediate counterpoint. "It's common for the murderer to report a body. It's the only remotely plausible way to avoid self-incrimination."

"How'd I kill him, then? There was no sign of injury. No blood. No blaster scorch. I *did* talk to him just prior, and he was fine. Either we're all liable to keel over dead without a moment's notice, or someone magicked him to death. And I'm certainly not a wizard."

There were grumbles around the periphery of the room, and the quarters were close enough that Eric caught the gist of a few. Namely, that, were Stooie Quatermain secretly a wizard, certain high-ranking Mars Navy and Mars Marine Corps officials would willingly dine upon portions of their dress uniforms.

"Magic doesn't take wizards," General Bob cut in. He shook his head. "Damned if I know thing one about the stuff, but I've had my security briefings. Too damn many, I thought until now."

"But *why* would I kill him?" Eric demanded. Heck, Uriela

had asked the same and Eric didn't have a great answer for her, either. "I mean, Kent Hershey was—I mean is... no, was—a great guy. He was trying to help me out."

"Help you with what, exactly?" Admiral DiBiase asked. Oh, now we were coming to the part where interrogators just asked every darned question that popped into their heads on the off chance the one sitting in the Unfortunate Chair couldn't come up with a consistent suite of lies on the spot and slipped. Pick. Pick. Pick away at a story, peeling away the coating of falsehood. The Hard Boiled Egg, Dad called it. You can't just eat one with the shell on, and the cops get in trouble for just smashing one. They had to carefully and meticulously introduce cracks, then excise the shell a bit at a time.

That was all well and good when dealing with *petty* criminals. But Eric had been raised by a better sort.

"He was a good guy. Warned me that there was a faction forming to try to force an exit to the bunker and not to fall in with them. He knows I—well, I mean knew that I—I mean... this is all confusing."

"Spit it out, Stooie," General Bob scolded. He sounded like other people's fathers.

"Well, I can tend to go along. I follow orders. I know it doesn't make me the best admiral; I hear the scuttlebutt. I know you all think it; say it when I'm not around. But I've got a clean service record and I'm a loyal son of Mars. Can we stop the witch hunt and start looking for the wizard that's got to be around here somewhere? Possibly in the room with us?"

A pall settled over the room. If glares were audible, the sound would have deafened them all.

General Bob put a stop to the silence with a grunt. "Well, I've got pointy-hats inbound. Vetted and as loyal as Mars Circle can promise." There was a quick, double-tap knock at the door, as if someone standing on the far side had been waiting for a cue. The supreme general raised his voice without taking his eyes off Eric. "C'mon in."

"You summoned me, Supreme General?" a tenor inquired. The speaker was spindly and hollow-cheeked, with a nose like a ski jump and eyes that sank into chasms on either side.

"Give Admiral Quatermain the once-over. Your way. Check his story."

"As you wish," the wizard responded, bowing low. When he rose, he addressed Eric directly. "Admiral, if you'd be so kind as to follow me."

Eric wasn't in a particular mood to be kind, but he welcomed the chance to leave that overstuffed kangaroo court.

In a supply closet nearby, two folding chairs had been set up facing one another. "Sit," the wizard directed Eric.

Eric sat.

The wizard took the seat opposite him.

"You will look me in the eye. You will not look away, blink, or attempt to block my intrusion into your mind."

"I'm not sure that's a good idea," Eric warned. "It's kind of a mess in there. You might get lost."

The wizard spared not a hint of a smile at Eric's lighthearted warning. Not that Eric expected him to beat a hasty retreat at such a limp and lame excuse. "I'll manage."

With that, the wizard widened his eyes and focused on Eric's.

After a resigned sigh, Eric obliged.

"I know it's been ages here, but for you... *What did we JUST talk about?*" Uriela demanded. She sat behind her ornate desk in the Village of Eternity Library, where Eric and his charge had just arrived.

Eric balled his fists and wished he had a better counterargument. "It was an interrogation."

"We had a plan. There were contingencies. You were supposed to show convincing evidence that events had taken place just as you described."

Eric flung a finger at the terrified shell of a mind that was following him around in a replica of the wizard's mortal body. "He jumped in with both feet. Snipping the little cord tethering him to his body was... it just... I made a reflexive decision, and I stand by it."

Uriela pointed a finger of her own at the hapless fellow, whom Eric now knew intuitively as Wizard Skogul Rasmussen of Mars Circle, Order of Hypnos. "You're *literally* standing by it. Eric, this can't keep happening!"

"I have a few questions," Eric informed her, changing the subject—slightly. "Can I—?"

"You snipped the wrong tether!" Uriela bellowed, rising from behind her desk. "You went into his mind and stayed there."

Eric's divine blood ran cold. "But..." He had no follow-up. Peering out into near-frozen external time, he could perceive Stooie Quatermain staring back at him.

"I've been frantically checking on the realms to see if anything's been lost or damaged in the transfer."

"And?" Eric's immortal stomach tied itself in knots.

Uriela huffed. "We appear to have been lucky."

Wizard Skogul raised a tentative finger. "If I might, I—"

"You may not!" Uriela snapped. The look she cast Eric defied him to overrule her. "Eric, you have moved us to a body with unknown political and professional affiliations. I suggest you get everything you need to switch impersonations and just let them discover that Stooie Quatermain was an impostor."

"But..."

"You can't go back. That body is a corpse now, and we don't do corpse stuff."

Eric remembered We Don't Do Corpse Stuff as something around Rule #17 of the Village of Eternity. Then again... "Rules were meant to be broken."

"Eric, focus. Wizard Skogul was one of several Martian Circle representatives—"

"Mars Circle," Eric interjected. If he couldn't be right about brain-hopping and body-discarding, he could at least get some verbiage correct.

"Actually," Wizard Skokgul chimed in, "both are considered acceptable as per the Edict of 2591."

"Shut it!" Uriela ordered.

"What should I do, then?" Eric asked. Clearly, Uriela had taken charge and had a plan of some sort.

Sitting back down, she huffed again, appearing placated for the moment. "You are Wizard Skogul Rasmussen, Order of Hypnos—"

"Our equivalent of the Order of Morpheus," the dead wizard supplied obsequiously.

"I suggest you report that you caught an impostor and that the threat is over."

"But then all the Martian government people would go back to governing Mars."

"Yes. Precisely. And you can go back to the Arete and explain being a forty-four-year-old bachelor with a peanut allergy and early onset arthritis to Charlotte and Jessie."

None of that sounded good. Not the explanation part. Not the sore joints. Certainly not a lifetime without peanut butter. Eric's favorite peanut butter spoon would be heartbroken!

"I'm not sure I like that plan."

"Eric..."

She knew him too well. "It'll be fine."

"ERIC..."

He wrapped an arm behind Skogul and shoved him forward. "You take our new guy and get him settled into the Villain Intervention Project."

"The WHAT?" Wizard Skogul exclaimed. "I'm no sort of—!"

"ERIC!" Uriela shouted. "I can't stop you from doing stupid things if you don't—"

Eric didn't hear the rest. His eyes were open. He found himself staring at a familiar body in borrowed clothes.

Part of him refused to believe that his body was dead. Shrink it. Stuff it in a pocket. Maybe Harmony could fix it later.

"Everything all right in there?" a marine sergeant called through the door.

Eric knew his plan wasn't great, but Uriela's wasn't entirely wrong, either. He needed to step out of the crosshairs long enough to plan his next dodge. "Yes. I've discovered the infiltrator.

"And slain him."

——

Enough was enough.

Why this tautological bromide popped into her head Charlotte couldn't say. She'd been brought up better than to lean so heavily into cliché. None of that mattered as she piled neatly folded laundry into a makeshift suitcase that had been meant to house a collapsible blaster rifle. Once the custom foam insets had been prised out, the shell gave all the storage of a TransGalactica carry-on bag.

Skirts. Blouses. Undergarments. Toiletries.

There came a rapping at her chamber door.

"I'm busy."

The door opened of its own accord. In stepped Mordecai in that stolen body of his. "That's fine. I don't mind."

"I do." A cardigan came unfolded as she laid it atop the piled clothes, prompting its immediate removal for a re-folding.

"You don't need to go after Eric. You'll end up like Carl, captured trying to do something noble and stupid and needing a rescue of your own—if you're lucky."

That smug, all-knowing look. That calm demeanor. He infuriated her. "And yet you moved heaven and Earth to rescue your friend Carl, and here you stand not lifting a finger over Eric."

"Carl's a nincompoop."

"Carl Ramsey is a grown man with decades of experience extricating himself from mess upon mess of his own creation."

Mordecai cleared his throat. "Point of order, the appearance of Carl being the galaxy's luckiest sonovabitch is due in no small part to our close personal association over the years. Sure, now and then he pulls a few rabbits out of a haberdashery and manages the improbable on his own, but that's the exception that proves the rule. Eric, on the other hand, is a walking time paradox waiting to happen. We'll find out he's had a rough go of it when Mars turns into a nineteenth-century cattle ranch out of the blue."

"I have a plan. And it's better than waiting to see whether Eric can manage to escape Mars on his own." Charlotte discovered that, now that she had her cardigan re-folded to her liking, she'd mussed her saffron blouse in the process of removing it from the suitcase to do so. Setting down the cardigan, she set about fixing the muddle she'd made of her blouse.

"Oh, really?"

"My mother has cultivated a vast array of contacts—"

"Indeed she has..."

"—over the course of a long and infamous career. I can have a travel ID whipped up in short order on my own recognizance without having to enlist my mother's aid. If you're willing to offer your services, a second ID can be forged with no additional delay."

"And what do you plan on doing once you get there?"

"I have my means."

"Sparta told me the book is missing."

Charlotte's face betrayed nothing. "She ought to look harder, then."

When she went to set the newly re-folded saffron blouse in the suitcase, she discovered a rumpled mess. Every last garment had been completely disheveled.

Mordecai smirked when she glared his way. "Nothing easier to delay than a perfectionist."

Stuffing the two folded garments atop their wrinkled compatriots, Charlotte slammed the suitcase shut. "You'll not catch me wallowing in dysfunction to the point of inaction. You won't stop me from going after him."

The youthful wizard blinked. Charlotte froze in place. "I was doing you a courtesy. You think I can't do any damn thing I like around here? Eric's a carpet wrinkle of an obstacle when he's around. Wizard Tiffany's a stray Plug'Em Block on the floor at night. You're nothing at all. The kid cares about you like you're family. You get him. No one else but me really knows him at all. You think I'm going to let you wander off the *Arete* in some damn fool attempt to sneak him off Mars out from under the noses of *real* wizards and have to explain how I let it happen when he gets back here all on his own?"

"This isn't about you!"

Mordecai bellowed a laugh. "Like it's all about *you*. I ruled Earth. Gave it up. Tore it down. Started the process of turning over a new forest. If it's not *all* about me, it mostly is. And of what's left over, Mr. I'm Five Years Younger Than I Ought To Be is a big chunk."

While she couldn't budge a muscle, not even to finish a step and touching the ground with her right foot, Charlotte found she could glare. "I'll agree to stop trying on one condition."

"No promises, but I'll hear you out."

"Oh, a promise is precisely what it will take. I want your word that if we receive evidence that Eric is in imminent danger, either in custody or as a fugitive, you'll personally take action to rescue him from Mars."

"On whose behalf I intervene is my own business. I'm not in the habit of letting friends or family suffer."

"Promise. Make it a vow or you'll have to explain to Jessica why her first officer is in suspended animation in her quarters. I won't stop trying short of those extremes."

Mort harrumphed as he turned to leave. "Spell will end before dinner. I'll warn Jessie to lock up any spare ships. If you want to extort *me*, you should have consulted the kid's father for help."

———

On one side of the table, beer flowed from pitcher to pint glasses. Across the way, two soda pops cracked open as a meal for four steamed before them all.

"You know, now that shit's winding down, we oughtta do stuff like this more often," Trebla declared. He offered a toast with his Peachberry Carbo-Cola. Jasmine obligingly lifted her Watermango. On the far side of the table, Mindy and Daphne joined in, resulting in a clink and a few hollow metallic clunks.

"Ain't nothing stoppin' us afore now, I s'pose," Mindy pointed out.

Jasmine snickered. "Other than working in different parts of a five-kilometer-long ship and pulling 20-hour shifts?"

"Or your preference for private entertainment," Daphne teased with half-closed eyes.

Mindy hastily cleared her throat. "All right, then. No need for cuttin' windows in the walls or nothin'."

Trebla finished a slurp of his spaghetti. "Tell ya what, I'm looking forward to life as a non-fugitive."

"At least in Earth and League space," Jasmine pointed out. She was in the process of cutting her noodles so short they'd almost have passed for rice and dousing the whole plate with grated Parmesan.

"Yeah, surprised ya girl Tiffany there could pull strings with the League."

Trebla snickered. "I don't know Aunt Tiff to pull strings. If anything, she tugged them taut, tied them off, and ordered them to stay pulled until further notice." The four shared a laugh over that. It was easier to laugh about Aunt Tiffany in her absence.

When the mirth died down, Jasmine made her move. They'd planned this out. She was point on all things diplomatic. "Heard you two were considering Meyang..."

Mindy nodded with her mouth full. "Yeah." She swallowed. "Wanted to see whether we oughtta head for Earth space to vote, now we's respectable citizens and all. But since it's all omni anyway, we're planning to hit up the captain soon as she's done nibbling her manicure over that brother of hers."

There were mixed opinions of Eric aboard the *Arete* on most matters. He was dangerous, unstable, and personable as fuck. The same, frankly, could be said about Mort. Well, maybe not the unstable part. In fact, there were barren planets out there less stable than Uncle Enzio with his new identity. He was like an antimatter cannon you could have a beer with. As for Eric, the only thing the crew agreed on nearly unanimously was that no one wanted to go traipsing around Mars looking to offer him a ride back to the *Arete*. For Trebla, it was a matter of personal safety.

Others would have been happy to have Eric perfectly safe and moving on to a new career anywhere else.

"Who do you two plan to vote for, if you don't mind discussing politics?" Daphne inquired. There was no full mouth for her. Food went in and simply vanished.

"Oh, no one," Jasmine replied cheerily. "Neither of us is eligible."

"All humans is, excepting Mars residents," Mindy reminded them.

Before Trebla could jump in, Jasmine raised a finger. "Ah, but legally speaking, I'm laaku. Native-born daughter of Phabian. *Iik padop yaaba.*"

"*Iik padop yaaba,*" Trebla echoed, self-conscious that she had less of an English accent than him. He'd learned Kejathi alongside English as a kid, but he'd operated in English most of his life.

"Damn. Never thought 'bout that. You kids planning a homecoming?"

"Nope!" Jasmine answered instantly and without a shred of hesitation. "But I'm not giving up my citizenship, either. Phabian didn't just have themselves a multi-year experiment in monarchy. Phabian didn't fracture into civil war. Thanks, I'll stick with my furry brothers and sisters." She gave Trebla a barefoot kick under the table, a lower-handed equivalent of a fist bump.

Trebla nodded his assent. It wasn't that hard to become an Earth citizen for a laaku. He knew his human history and his civics—well, he did in the pre-imperial and imperial regimes, anyway—and he spoke fluent English. "Well, we'll miss you gals. How... uh... how *long* you expecting to be gone?"

Jasmine caught his eye. The tiniest of nods affirmed that he'd been tactful. Jasmine had tried to bet him a hundred terras that they weren't planning on a return trip at all. Things were changing on Meyang, and for the better, if one were either an exmundiate Earth citizen or a disavowed rebel terrorist. Both were now eligible for permanent residency and citizenship.

Trebla hadn't taken the bet.

"Aw, couple'a weeks, tops," Mindy replied with a shrug. "Hiking, mostly. Area Daph's fam is from ain't much to visit. Chem factories and a tram hub. We checked. Naw, just gonna see sights. Breathe some authentic air."

"Maybe get her fur done," Daphne joked, running a hand over her partner's scalp.

"Great. Yeah. You do that," Trebla told them, his relief palpable.

Daphne was far too keen-eyed. "You didn't think we'd move there, did you?" Jasmine's next kick under the table was a shin-stinger. "Meyang is my birthplace. But it's also a primitive hellscape without even a proper delicatessen and with more bullfighting arenas than omni channels."

Mindy nodded. "I said weeks, but we's bringin' our own wings. Shine wears off, we lay ions."

Daphne tittered self-consciously. "You know... truth be told... when you invited us to dinner, we both thought it was a goodbye."

"Huh?" Jasmine scrunched her brow. "You mean... wait, *us* leaving? Fuck no. *Iik padop yaaba's* fine for Ancestors' Walk and all, but you'd have to open our quarters to hard-vac to get me off the *Arete*. Vacation in the arboretum. Retire to maybe doing odd jobs. When I die, leave my carcass in the columniation stream of the Annihilation Particle Cannon."

"I'm with her," Trebla clarified when eyes turned his way following the diatribe.

Maybe he'd get antsy cooped up on the *Arete* after a while. Maybe he'd need time away. But he wasn't sure how he'd enjoy free time without Jasmine at his side. Trebla had grown up a spacer. Planetside life had nipped at his ankles until he found some way back to the Black Ocean. He doubted a single lifetime would be long enough to weary him of a ship this monstrous and wonderful and wonderfully monstrous.

Mindy lifted a half-empty glass. "Now, then. Looks like we's all stuck with one another for the foreseeable, eh? To peace."

"TO PEACE!"

The back ways and in-betweens of the *Arete* were larger than most of the crew realized. The ones who knew better worked in Logistics or Engineering, and Engineering hadn't been invited to this meeting. Only two in attendance weren't ratatoret.

Aubrey sat with her knees tucked to her chest atop a flat cushion. Her hair brushed the ceiling until she pulled it back into a ponytail.

The other non-ratatoret reclined on her shell, supported on a custom low-ride grav sled. Unlike Aubrey, who lurked at the back where she didn't block anyone's view, Uom'pe had a place of honor up with Tippitak on the small presentation stage.

But this was Makket's show.

The tiny amphitheater was just large enough to accommodate the whole Logistics department. Other than using the public areas of the ship, it was the only finished portion of the *Arete* that would. And it was the perfect venue for the Logistics Department Quarterly Update.

"Welcome-everyone-thank-you-for-finding-time-in-your-schedules-to-be-here." Makket paused for a titter of laughter throughout the amphitheater. He'd cleared everyone's daily planners himself. "As-the-Harvest-Quarter-draws-to-a-close-I'd-like-to-bring-everyone-up-to-speed-on-the-department's-status-and-a-look-ahead-into-our-plans-for-the-future-I-now-turn-things-over-to-my-silky-furred-bride-Tippitak-for-the-financials."

Tippitak bowed and accepted a round of chitters and whistles (and one pair of clapping human hands). "Thank-you-Thank-you-all-The-*Arete*-has-made-large-financial-strides-this-quarter-Sensing-that-the-assassination-of-many-Martian-officials-might-bring-a-quick-end-to-the-war-we-took-short-positions-on-several-defense-megacorps-While-the-intended-coup-took-place-on-the-wrong-planet-our-ruse-to-help-convince-Earth-that-we-expected-a-Martian-collapse-resulted-in-a-considerable-windfall-With-the-dissolution-of-Imperial-Technical-Systems-and-the-stock-price-collapse-of-Destro-Fleet-Services-we-have-a-digital-stock-portfolio-of-upward-of-six-billion-terras-primarily-reinvested-in-terramancy-stocks.'

Uom'pe took her cue, but the transition from laser-speed to glacial was jarring nonetheless. "We. Have started. Contracts. With several. Ship supply. Companies. Wherever. We travel. In Earth. Or League. Of Independent. Planet territory. We can. Fully restock. All essential. And nonessential. And luxury. Supplies. Rest. Assured. That my. Dinner offerings. Will only. Benefit. From this. Increased. Variety. Of ingredients."

It was a fool who thought the old tesud only cooked around the ship. Tippitak took the credit. And in fairness, she'd authorized all the stock transactions. But it had been the tortoise who'd come up with the idea to bet against the arms suppliers ahead of ending their little war, and which stocks would suffer most and quickest. Truly, waiting for stews to cook gave anyone plenty of time to theorize and strategize.

Makket stepped to the fore after a quick shake of one of Uom'pe's fingers. She then piloted her grav sled out of the venue. After all, only so many recipes could be allowed to remain unattended all afternoon.

"Excellent-news-all-around-And-now-without-further-ado-I'd-like-to-share-the-centerpiece-of-our-stock-windfall-expenditures." He paused for eight-tenths of a second for dramatic effect. "I-give-you-Smalltown!"

A holograph exploded to life on stage. Concealed in the ceiling, only the eight workers who'd helped install it would even have known it was there. The scene depicted the *Arete*, but translucent. All the nominally inhabited regions of the ship had been left blank, merely indicated by color and a legend in the corner to help everyone reference the schematic. But between all those big spaces, the unused—no, *wasted*—space teemed.

"I-have-contracted-with-the-esteemed-architectural-firm-Nittocob-Rapanak-and-Associates-to-design-a-fully-functional-and-nearly-independent-city-within-the-interstitial-spaces-of-the-*Arete*-I-predict-that-a-peacetime-*Arete*-will-become-a-hub-of-medical-tourism-and-safe-transactional-commerce-within-the-security-auspices-of-our-venerable-haathee-host."

As Makket spoke, the schematic rotated and zoomed, offering extensive views of the planned construction.

"As-you-can-see-We-will-have-extensive-transportation-housing-and-personal-services-provided-There-are-schools-daycare-and-sporting-facilities-for-children-Private-eating-and-cooking-hubs-A-temple-to-Womomgloo-A-secondary-holotheater-Every-member-of-the-Logistics-Department-will-receive-private-personal-quarters-No-more-communal-bunking."

A cheer greeted that announcement.

But the enthusiasm wasn't unanimous. A large head hung at the back of the amphitheater.

It was too much for Makket to take. "Aubrey-You-are-a-valued-member-of-the-Logistics-Department-Did-you-stop-to-consider-that-once-Uom'pe-left-there-was-no-reason-for-me-not-to-switch-to-ratatoret-and-be-done-with-this-presentation-ten-minutes-earlier-if-I-didn't-intend-to-include-you?"

"Sorry," Aubrey replied. "I've been practicing."

Makket shook his head emphatically. "You're-missing-my-point-entirely-We-have-carved-out-a-special-unit-of-housing-with-the-largest-available-ceiling-height-of-1.4-meters-You-will-have-your-own-suite-with-a-human-sized-mattress-and-shower-Unless-you-*prefer*-living-in-the-communal-bunks."

In truth, it worried Makket that she might. A number of the department workers had taken to nestling up against her in the oversized bunk on the floor, an arrangement that seemed popular with both.

Tears in her eyes, the Logistics Department's Chief Freight Handling Assistant for Shelves Two and Three smiled. "Thank you."

The comm connected on schedule. That was the one bit of this that had gone off without a hitch.

In an ideal galaxy (one in which Carl Ramsey had never found himself living), he would have had Eric and Jessie here for this. Instead, he had to settle for a long-lost sister-in-law and... well, another sister-in-law, he supposed.

On the wall, the whole *Squadron 33 1/3* clan appeared. Roddy and Shoni waved in unison, Roddy using a hand with a can of Earth's Preferred in it for lack of any hand without one

Yomin and Jean lounged in a papasan chair, hinting that their on-again, off-again "thing" was currently in the "on" position. Ozzy had one of Roddy's beers, toasting the screen with it. He'd kept growing his hair out, longer than his mother's by now, and worn loose, rock-star style.

Front and center, right where Carl knew the wall controls in their New Garrelon home to be, was Amy.

"Hey, babe!" Carl called out to her.

"Hey, babe, yourself. Where's Eric?"

Carl pursed his lips. "So. You heard."

"Damn right, I heard," Amy snapped. She spared a smile for Jamie and Sofia. "Hi. So nice to finally meet you. Just a minute while I murder your brother in front of you."

Jamie put her feet up on her brother's couch. "Oh, don't mind me. Glad to see the kid's been getting enough murder in his life."

"Eric's fine," Carl assured his wife. "It's like all those times where we lost him in a shopping mall or at a park or at a concert venue or—"

"It's nothing like any of those," Amy countered. "He's missing and in danger."

"Look, I can't talk about where Eric may or may not be right now, but—"

"He's on Mars," Amy cut in. "I've already spoken to Jessie about this. *She* didn't mind telling her mother where her oldest son was last seen."

"Yeah, about Jessie, she—"

"Will be along when she's able. She's got a starship to run and a brother to find. You don't have any excuse."

Carl raised a finger. "I was being held captive by the former Earth Government."

"Your own damn fault!"

Behind him, Sofia whispered to her wife. "(I can see why he likes her.)"

"Lay off him, Mom," Ozzy said with a smile. "Eric's got it all under control. No worries."

"How's school?" Carl asked, widening his grin to its maximum.

"Heading back in the morning. I've got a security detail, now."

"Super. Super. So, everyone. I think I've mentioned that my sister Jamie died when I was a kid. At the time I didn't *know* I was lying, but—" He stepped aside and swept both arms to the woman who raised a pint of Grosstet's beer in salute.

"It really *is* nice to meet you," Amy returned, almost as if there was a switch somewhere on her that swapped between dealing with him and with the rest of the galaxy. But there wasn't. He checked every square centimeter of her on the regular, and there was no sign of one.

"I'm honestly surprised you're real," Roddy claimed. "But I can't see the scam. So... welcome to being alive!"

"You know, I kept tabs on Brad a little over the years. It's a little surreal seeing all you dossiers interactively." Jamie tried to hide it, but Carl could tell how nervous she was, even after two beers with a third in progress.

"So, what have *you* been up to all this time?" Amy inquired, fighting not to turn the subject back to Eric. Carl could see it in the lines on her face.

Jamie sighed. "My own thing. Took a while. Too long. It would have been embarrassing to come back to ARGO space in a stolen eyndar ship after the war, only to prove this knucklehead went and avenged me prematurely."

Carl wagged a finger in his elder sister's direction. "Hey, when you finally *do* kick it, you're pre-avenged."

"Only if she gets killed by the ghost of an eyndar pilot you shot down," Sofia pointed out.

But this was no time for semantics. "Details, schmetails." With no wizard around to counter his ploy, that level of debate brilliance stood unchallenged.

"Where's Trebsie?" Shoni asked. "I thought he was going to be here."

Why should he? No one invited him. This party was too crowded as it stood. "He sends his apologies. Jessie keeps him pretty busy, you know, responsible for all the systems on an alien warship and all."

There was a problem with reunions, a balancing act this gathering had already stumbled from on two different counts. First off, you couldn't have this many people to either side of a comm panel and get any meaningful interactions. "Heartfelt" didn't do big audiences, and depth required time that would hog the stage with everyone else mere spectators. Secondly, frequency.

If you talk to someone every day, you talk about work or school or what was on the latest omni feed you both like.

Knock that back to a couple months, you get some real catching up. Maybe even as far back as a year.

Much beyond that, and you're getting to know strangers. "How was that hobby of yours?" turns into "What do you do for a living again?" or "Who was that?" when hearing names of people central to their lives.

And that's just how the rest of the comm went.

Asking about people who weren't there. Reminders of who everyone knew. It was half Ancient Family Mythology, half blind date.

Then, mercifully, a round of goodbyes and promises to keep in touch.

"They seem nice," Sofia commented once the panel had gone dark.

"It's not your fault," Jamie told Carl. "They've only got your outdated stories of me to go by."

"I know."

A heavy silence lingered. "You're mad at me."

"Damn right I'm mad at you!" Carl snapped. "You stole your damn life from me!"

Jamie hung her head. "I know."

Carl fumed. "First you ran off to Earth Navy. Then... whatever *this* is." He gestured to her in her Pirate Captain's Casual travel attire. "And you couldn't sneak in a quick 'hey, I'm alive, keep it to yourself'?"

"I didn't want to ruin the life you'd built."

"Newsfeed: you're what I spent most of my life unruining it *from*."

Jamie swallowed. "I'm... I don't know what to... I mean... I'm... sorry?"

Finally. Carl let his pent-up anger seep out his toes and presumably into some H-tech floor drain gizmo that cleared up emotional waste products. "Apology accepted. I'm too old for carrying grudges. Must go double for you, you old relic. C'mon. Let's grab a beer and I'll kick your ass at pool again."

Jamie wiped her eyes as she got up. "Wow. That's a throwback. And you've never beaten me at pool."

"I was eleven last time we played. I've gotten better."

Sofia trailed after them as the Ramsey siblings departed Carl's quarters. "You used to let him drink beer when he was eleven? ... You just mean the playing pool, right? ... You didn't seriously...? ... Jamie, what were you thinking?"

Carl shared a smirk with his sister.

Chuck would have laughed at him for getting drunk that underage.

Becky would have laid a "serves ya right" on him for a hangover.

Jamie was the one who'd carried his scrawny, bony, gangly ass home when he was stupid. She was the one who'd taught him the latest do-it-yourself hangover cures.

And she was about to learn what a life playing dive bars did for a guy's pool skills.

━━━

She'd lost count around eight. The whole galaxy wanted Jessie on a comm, and she was beginning to feel like it was a worse fate than everyone wanting her in front of a firing squad with her ship torn down in the name of military science. Even picking and choosing, filtering most and delegating many, her list of meetings grew faster than she could get the meetings over with.

These days, Jessie's ready room looked almost professional. Behind her, Haathee Federation and Arete flags dangled from poles, flanking a flatpic gallery of the vessel's triumphs. Her desktop was clear of anything except the backside of a terminal and her own sweaty, interlaced hands. Of course, if the camera could see three hundred and sixty degrees, it would have spotted the wheeled coat rack with her jacket hanging askew, a crate of Dozy-Ohs she'd been enjoying lately as a snack, and the trays with both her breakfast and lunch remnants waiting for Logistics to take away.

Usually, Logistics was more on the ball than this.

However, Jessie didn't have time to dwell on the mild inconvenience of smelling both pancake syrup and melted cheddar as she argued with Assistant Director Martha Mayhew of Earth Interstellar.

"Yeah. I get that. And I *appreciate* the offer. And I also

appreciate the fact that you're not doing this as a favor; you're following a fucking *order*."

The assistant director had a face designed by committee to deliver bad news. She was stern, cold, and impersonal. She held a press conference with Jessie as the only attendee. "While I may have been instructed by Dictator Bell to grant pardons to your crew, I cannot simply wave a magic wand. I need a full list of names and birth ID numbers for everyone in order to have the appropriate records updated."

"And I have a majority of my crew who think this is a honeypot operation you're running behind the dictator's back to document them for later punitive action once Dictator Bell hands over power to the new government."

"What kind of pardon do you think this is?"

"The convenient kind from your end. You've got a mandate. Follow it."

That implacable face didn't show any hint of the fury and frustration that must have lurked behind those eyes. "I cannot allow anyone to merely claim to have served aboard your vessel and expect carte blanche for every crime they may have committed."

Several factors played into Jessie's reluctance.

Most of the Logistics Department was content to take their chances with evading arrest if ever they departed the *Arete*. They worried more about reprisals against family members, which Jessie totally understood.

There was also the matter of not being able to contact Aunt Tiffany, which promised to get Jessie what she wanted without caving to some high-level bureaucrat like Mayhew.

Mostly, however, there was a quirk to the blanket pardon that Jessie simply couldn't overlook. It was granted to everyone aboard the *Arete*, and Eric wasn't here. Until she could be sure her brother was covered by the pardon, she wasn't giving a centimeter.

"Sorry. Consult with your people. Find a better solution. Get back to me. I've got other comms lined up behind you."

"You can't possibly expect—"

Jessie ended the comm before she discovered the precise nature of Assistant Director Mayhew's outrage.

Mom and Dad would be on a comm with Aunts Jamie and Sofia by now. Probably half the band, too. Who knew who else might pop in on Mom's end once they heard Dad would be there.

Blinking red indicators in her incoming comm log warned of secretaries, personal assistants, and junior officers lying in wait, ready to hand Jessie over to a superior as soon as she gave the signal she was available.

Who next?

The Earth Navy Admiralty?

Phabian Sentientarian Services?

The Galactic Alliance of Seekers—whom Jessie was only planning to humor out of curiosity. What could a bunch of religious ideologues want with *her*? There'd damn well better not have been a religion popping up around Grosstet again.

Then, Jessie spotted it.

Harmony.

How had Harmony Richelieu, her own Chief Medical Officer, not gotten through the comm blocks she had in place to avert days lost to distraction?

Jessie immediately connected.

"*Oh! Captain. One sec!*" Medic Daschel exclaimed.

The voice switched. "*Jess, can you come down to Med Bay?*"

"Is it urgent?"

"*It's... time-sensitive. Please?*"

Please? Who was this? Certainly not the Harmony Jessie knew. Whatever it was, it sounded more important than the grocery list of annoyances her comm queue held in store for her.

Jessie whooshed through the bridge, exchanging perfunctory salutes with the duty shift, and took a quick lift ride. She was in Med Bay in under a minute.

"What's the problem?"

Harmony had her back to the door, as did Britney, leaning over the doctor's shoulder and looking at *something*. Both turned, showing off dopey expressions of adoration.

Jessie's eyes went wide.

The swaddled bundle in Harmony's arms was... a baby!

"But... but... whose? How...?" The newborn appeared human. Pale. Pink. Eyes squeezed shut. Only the face visible. A quick inventory of the potential mothers wasn't a long list. Jasmine. Aubrey. A pair of maybes. Mindy would have Daphne's claws in her throat for sure if it was hers. Medic Daschel—Britney—didn't look like a woman who'd just given birth and hadn't struck her as particularly pregnant recently.

Jessie wasn't the only newcomer to Med Bay. Right on her heels, a pair of bare feet slapped a miniature stampede past her. "Is she here? Is that her?"

"Yes, pumpkin. This is your new baby sister."

Xrista let out a squeal and raced over to a low chair just her size. Harmony gingerly handed over the baby and showed the girl how to properly cradle one.

"Sister?" Jessie echoed belatedly. "But... you weren't pregnant, were you?"

Harmony worked out. She and Jessie crossed paths in the gym with some regularity. Plus, they saw one another in daily briefings that the doctor almost always made time for. How could something like this have snuck past her?

"I wasn't. I never *have been*," Harmony told Jessie as she led the conversation out the door while Britney supervised the cooing.

Jessie glanced over at Xrista, then back to Harmony. "Family resemblance?"

"Three of a kind, now."

Jessie lowered her voice below even the baby-sleeping-nearby level she'd been employing. "Can't you lose your medical license for this sort of thing? It's cloning. Right?"

"Jess, I could theoretically lose that license over half of what I do on a daily basis. I've experimented on live patients—including myself—with unsanctioned alien technology. What I used for Xrista was a simple variant of the process that led to the births of my sisters. Two genetic mothers is actually *harder* than a single parent. And riskier. Both girls are perfectly healthy. I made sure of that. They even carry the same genetic fixes I've had over the years—nothing outwardly noticeable, just some recessive risk factors that would have been ticking time bombs."

"How could you not tell me?"

"Habit. Not even my mothers know about Xrista's origin. Esper thinks I paid some poor, starving PhD student to donate. Karen assumes I got knocked up by someone I'm embarrassed to admit sleeping with. The only ones I've come out and told explicitly are Britney and the new godmother."

"Who's—?" Jessie wasn't dumb enough to finish that sentence she'd started by reflex. She blinked to clear her eyes. "What's her name?"

"Blessica."

Jessie cocked her head. Martian names would never make sense to her. But she gave herself credit for not cringing visibly. "Never heard that one."

"A squoosh of 'Blessing named after Jessica.' Hope you don't mind me not consulting you first."

Tears in her eyes, Jessie found herself already hugging Harmony.

━━━

A recent discovery of Small Cooking had been the peanut butter cookie. Easy to make. Highly illegal in most human communities —though he'd come to understand that a great many wonderful products were. His version of the recipe had required some advanced baking techniques to get an even texture throughout a cookie far larger than the ones the instructions presumed.

Each the size of a dining lounge plate, Grosstet had spent the morning making six hundred of them. With a mere two hundred and fifty or so remaining, he worried that his indulgence might spoil his enjoyment of his upcoming dinner.

But the whole point of today was to allow worries to seep from him.

Carl was safe.

The human war might be ending or might not, depending whom he asked.

Makket had asked permission to build an entire city in parts of the *Arete* that Grosstet largely pretended didn't exist.

Jessie and Mordecai had returned triumphant.

But not all was well.

Eric was still missing, unaccounted for after the recent deception and subsequent rescue mission.

Four bodies had been disposed of without ceremony, victims of that successful scheme.

Grosstet had needed cheering up. His plan had been more than mere cookies.

He'd enlisted the help of the ship's computer and determined the areas through which the most foot traffic passed. Of course, the easiest two answers had been the hangar and the communal dining hall. But he didn't want to be *in the way*. Once he apprised the computer of his goal, an eventual winner became Junction 141.

Located along a footpath that one might cross venturing between any of six popular and semi-popular destinations, nearly a quarter of the crew passed through daily.

"GOOD DAY, NABAPTIK! CARE FOR A COOKIE?" Grosstet held out his guest platter, upon which numerous crumb-sized micro-cookies awaited snacking.

"Why-thank-you-but-I-was-just-on-my-way-to-Med-Bay-I-don't-think-it's-terribly-serious-but-Chinochin-is-trying-to-crack-down-on-workplace-carelessness-and-I-believe-that-he-thinks-making-us-report-even-the-most-minor-of-injuries-to-Dr-Richelieu-may-act-as-a-deterrent."

"ARE YOU FEELING WELL?"

"I-got-my-tail-caught-between-two-cardboard-packing-units-whose-contents-did-not-exceed-two-kilograms-While-I-admit-to-letting-out-a-startled-yip-I-was-unable-to-convince-Chinochin-that-I'd-suffered-no-injury-in-the-process."

Quick math gave the haathee some idea of the feathery payloads between which Nabaptik had been—well, to call it "crushed" would be a vast exaggeration. "IF YOU HAVE A WISH FOR COOKIES UPON COMPLETING YOUR PUNISHMENT TRIP TO DR. HARMONY, YOU ARE WELCOME TO RETURN. BETTER YET, TAKE A FEW WITH YOU."

"Thank-you-so-much-You-know-what-I-think-I'll-take-you-up-on-that-offer-Have-an-excellent-remainder-of-your-day-Commodore."

Grosstet grinned. He loved having a title.

Trebla came through with a laden grav sled and no time to chitchat, but he accepted a few small cookies.

Charlotte declined his offer and warned him to be careful. The cookies were apparently deadly to a significant percentage of humans. She planned to hold him responsible if anyone got sick from them.

That warning seemed to carry little weight with DeAndre, who stayed for a few minutes before a comm from Lisa summoned him away to duty.

Duty. Grosstet had had duties once.

Around the *Arete*, he pitched in where he felt needed. Mostly, he oversaw. Jessie ran the ship. Makket moved everything around inside it. Harmony took care of everyone's health. Mordecai had taken over responsibility for magic, and despite his distinct social preference for Eric, he *did* feel noticeably more confident in Mordecai knowing what he was doing. Even without knowing a toot of magic himself, Grosstet could pick up on the difference in confidence and... it was hard to describe. Eric disappeared the moment one stopped looking his way. Mordecai filled rooms before even entering them, and his presence lingered once he was gone.

As his cookie supply dwindled and the promise of a proper meal grew increasingly pointless, Grosstet realized the core of his issue.

Loneliness was merely a new symptom.

He was herdsick.

Home was so, *so* far away. Upon first arriving in this part of the galaxy, everything had been new and novel and exciting. He'd been the center of attention, and adulation plus awe was a passable substitute for connection. Then, getting mixed up with Jessie and her ever-growing crew of small people, everything had turned righteous and dangerous and... still exciting. Sometimes sad. Actually, it got sad any time he stopped to think about it. But now... well, the excitement was drying up.

He missed Eric, surely. Eric was a good friend and the only one who understood haathee.

That was another factor.

He hadn't carried on a conversation in his birth language in years.

But home and herd were impossibly far away. Even with the astral travel option, it would likely have taken years. Just fewer years than it had taken getting this far from the homeworld.

And so, Grosstet packed up his remaining cookies, leaving the smaller cookies for whoever stumbled across them, and headed for an early bedtime.

Charlotte rapped smartly on the door of an erstwhile disused storage room. When no response came from inside after what she deemed a polite wait, she rapped harder.

"*Occupied,*" Sparta replied through the door.

Allowing her palm to be analyzed by the door panel's haathee thumb scanner, Charlotte overrode the door controls.

She marched inside to find Sparta crosslegged on the floor with her back to the entrance. Crates piled around the walls of the chamber, stacked three humans high, gave the appearance of precariousness that she trusted Makket and his people had not allowed to remain actually dangerous.

"Had I not already been aware you were in here, I shan't have knocked."

"Mort's not here," Sparta told her without turning.

"You may be shocked to learn that the majority of this vessel takes orders from me. I'm rarely caught unawares by the location of individuals I may be seeking. Wizard Mordecai is availing himself of the holovid theater. Presumably, an advanced showing of *Five Faces to Punch* did not appeal to your tastes."

Still, the oracle didn't so much as glance at Charlotte from the corner of her eye. "I don't speak Kejathi. I'll wait for the dubbed version."

"While you wait, I have a task for you."

Sparta exhaled, tightroping the line between cleaning meditative breathing and exasperation. "This is the part where you pull rank on me since Mort isn't here to chase you off."

"Indeed. Despite your suitor's warnings and admonitions, I have word through questionable sources that the Martian Dictatorial Cabal have eliminated a spy. That's pretense enough for me to get there and be ready to abscond with Eric the instant he pokes his head from the hole they're all hiding in."

Charlotte's theory was that Eric had been caught up in the security lockdown and couldn't find a morally acceptable way to enact an exit. A dead body in that cloister could either be a sign that he'd gotten cornered and called out or had bent his principles enough to justify a murder for his own freedom.

Finally, Sparta turned. Her whole face had been painted in black and white, a pattern Charlotte didn't recognize. But the medium appeared to be stage makeup, if she was any judge. "Can this wait? This would have been my grandmother's birthday."

Charlotte set her jaw. Times like this, she wished she possessed the innate gifts of the other wizards of the *Arete*. Eric sniffed magic like a bloodhound. He casually noticed things Charlotte couldn't see despite her best efforts. Mordecai, by all accounts, could read runes like prose—Hemingway, at that. Even Sparta was both more powerful and subtle than she.

There was every chance that the oracle's face was *not*, in fact, presently painted for some manner of séance. Or hadn't been a moment prior, at any rate.

Better to be thought heartless than made a fool.

"I plan to depart within the hour. It's been three days since Mordecai humiliated me. I cannot abide any longer."

"Let me guess. There's a little over an hour left of that laaku action holo?"

Charlotte kept mum.

"Look. I can't just 'find' Eric. Mort carves his own riverbed as he goes. Eric is a bucket of water that won't flow downhill. But it's the same problem trying to read either one."

"Try," Charlotte insisted. If there was one thing Mother had hammered into her as a girl, it was that giving up without making one's best effort was simply unacceptable.

With a huff, Sparta shut her eyes and bowed her head.

This time, Charlotte could feel the arcane forces at work. Gravity wasn't strictly downward. Time proceeded at a slight angle. Places and probabilities and memories overlapped like a stack of printed flatpics on translucent plastic.

And she wasn't the one experiencing visions.

Sparta gasped and opened her eyes.

"What! What is it?" Charlotte demanded.

It took a moment of panting breath for Sparta to gather herself, shaking her head in what might have been either an attempt to clear it or to blow off Charlotte's question. "Nothing. Just... got a little lost in the netherworld."

Charlotte had seen her share of horrors. Moreover, she'd witnessed the effects on others more times than she cared to recall. The oracle had seen something. "Tell me."

"False vision. You're better off not hearing it. It takes experience to tell the difference."

"Tell. Me. NOW."

Had it come to violence in that moment, Charlotte weighed her chances rashly. An all-out effort to thwart Sparta's magical defenses, followed up with a manual pummeling. In no universe could she both overcome Sparta's powers and continue to make use of them.

However, as a purely psychological ploy, one of the pair was highly more conflict averse. Sparta relented. "I saw Eric's body."

Charlotte's blood ran cold. She felt faint.

"Told you!" Sparta had her arms around Charlotte's shoulders before the *Arete's* second in command could faint. Thin, bony hands guided Charlotte to a seat. "But it can't be Eric. Someone *else* saw Eric's body, and if it were really him, I wouldn't be able to. You follow? It's like... it's... you know when pirates leave a booby-trapped ship for Earth Navy to find?"

Charlotte felt numb inside and chose to nod in the affirmative rather than debate the differences between holovid pirates and actual starfaring buccaneers. No right-thinking pirate gave up a vessel—not to mention the expense of explosives—just to throw off investigators. Run. Hide. Sell. Spend. Kill too many naval officers, damage too many vessels and the mightiest fleet in this half of the galaxy would redouble their efforts.

But for now, the analogy seemed not in want of technical accuracy so much as getting to a point.

"Well, if someone actually killed Eric, I'd get a snap of clarity. His path would be ended, his past set in stone. Right now, everything he does is written in faint pencil, including that body I saw. I don't know what it means. YOU don't know what it means. But I'm confident Eric is still alive. Is that enough for you?"

Charlotte nodded as her circulation continued to recover. "If you'll satisfy my curiosity, where *did* you see a body?"

"Some military safehouse under New Vancouver. Now... it's *still* my late grandmother's birthday, and I may have said a few things to her on her deathbed, so this isn't an easy conversation to get started. If you don't mind, I'd like to get back to trying."

"Of course. Naturally."

The *Hummingbird* was waiting for Charlotte in the hangar. One among the many, many little vessels the *Arete* had purloined in its pirate-hunting adventures, it had nothing special to recommend it except that it was unremarkable, would hardly be missed, and she'd prepacked her luggage aboard it before tracking down Sparta for a destination.

Oh, and Charlotte had watched the flight operations holo-instructions for the make and model three times and stored a replica of the performance in her mental bookshop.

Switches: flicked.

Numbers: within appropriate ranges.

Buttons: pressed in sequence.

Comm: "Bridge, this is Commander Webber. Open the hangar airlock."

Hmm. In the holo, there had been lights around the comm panel to indicate to whom she was speaking. Actually, a great number of lights and readouts had all gone blank.

No.

It couldn't.

She hadn't even buckled into the pilot's chair, and she was already getting out of it. Back to the boarding ramp, which wouldn't open via the controls.

It opened on its own, metal and pistons groaning in protest.

"You!"

"Yeah, me," Mordecai The Brown replied testily. "Thought we had a deal."

"An ultimatum in no way constitutes a deal, and, at any

rate, that was the contingency for your involvement. How did you even know to find me here? Isn't your holovid still running?"

"You owe me getting ahold of the dubbed version when it comes out. Sparta came running into the theater like some kind of kabuki demon, spouting off about you going to Mars by yourself."

"Even you have to admit it's been too long. Eric doesn't do well on his own. By now, he'll be making bad decisions atop bad decisions in some vain effort to cancel them all out like overcomplicated mathematics. He needs me."

"Maybe he doesn't." Before Charlotte could protest, with expert timing, he added, "But maybe he does. He sure as hell doesn't need *me*. I don't make his decisions for him. But I also can't let you go running off half-cocked and getting yourself killed. He'd never forgive me."

"I won't stop trying," Charlotte promised, clutching the opening of the *Hummingbird,* despite a vow carved in marble that it wouldn't be going anywhere without Mordecai's leave. "You'll have to keep me prisoner to stop me."

"Or... hear me out... I can send you after him fully armed and capable of looking after yourself."

Charlotte retreated a step into the ship's cramped interior. "You're not suggesting what I think. Are you?"

Mordecai shrugged. "Get off that little rowboat. Think it over. If you're willing to risk death to go bring Eric back, why not go full gusto?"

⸺

Charlotte dined alone in her quarters. Or rather, she dined with her worries, swirling emotions, and possibilities, and the lot of them crowded out any possibility of guests in the vast, vacant quarters she ought to have been sharing with Eric.

She had just enough spare pique to wonder, as she considered the carbonara on her plate, that someone ought to have a word with the whoever was in charge of procurement these days about the surplus of spaghetti aboard. While a versatile pasta, there were limits to the varieties one could tolerate before the underlying noodles became tedious.

Oh, if only Eric were here to consult. Not only would he talk her out of taking up Mordecai's offer of dark library privileges, he'd have wonderfully unhinged ideas about how to liven up this dreary meal.

Doom kept an hourglass but never a day planner.

Somewhere, presumably on Mars, likely in the very bunker in which Sparta had denied his demise, Eric was running out of time. For a man who gallivanted through fields of sundials and flapped the arms of a clock like insect wings, the concept of not having unlimited time struck a dissonant chord in Charlotte's mind.

But how soon? How long would Sparta's vision remain errant? Eric habitually underestimated his personal peril. The longer Charlotte debated, the more chance he had to meet an unhappy end. But the longer she waited, the better chance of good news as well. Fate's course had been set, and she knew not what planet the stellar winds would guide his vessel toward, unpiloted.

Mordecai's offer was a slow poison in her veins. Her own beating heart was pumping the toxin toward vital organs.

Eric had been vague about the *Tome of Bleeding Thoughts*. He avoided speaking its name outside the Village of Eternity. Supposedly, it was a wildfire in the mind. He was more gifted than Charlotte could even imagine. The same went for Mordecai. The only other one Eric had been certain had read the dreaded book was Wizard Tiffany. The librarian was twice as brash and brazen as Mother and, by all accounts, nearly the equal of her mentor.

How could Charlotte dare read what they had read?

She envisioned the smoldering eyes of Wizard Yarzzi and could feel the heat rising in her own at the mere image.

The door chimed, freeing Charlotte from her solitude and the latter half of her dinner as well. "Enter."

It was Eric's simpering father outside. He stepped in without a hint of decorum or respect for her privacy. "Hey, heard you had a run-in with Mort in the hangar."

"Gossip spreads quicker than I like on the *Arete*, despite my efforts to discourage it."

Carl sauntered over to the dining table and joined her. Normally, the pair of seats precluded guests, but with Eric gone, Charlotte was less one buffer against people. "Don't worry about it. I'm easy to talk to. Can't blame people for doing what comes naturally."

She didn't feel it was a good use of her rhetorical arsenal to point out that various churches and governments had been doing precisely that since before recorded history began. "What Wizard Mordecai and I spoke of is none of your concern."

"Yeah, but you not breaking my kid's heart by getting yourself killed kind of involves me. Whether you like it or not. And, since I'm already involved, why not bounce some ideas off me? I'm great at figuring convoluted personal shit out."

For want of becoming a cliché, this man could have been her father-in-law. And despite every shred of instinct life had instilled in her arguing that it was impossible, evidence suggested that Carl's claim was more true than not.

"Are you familiar with a certain book?"

Carl twitched a smile, gone as quick as it appeared. "Not directly. But yeah."

"It would likely burn my mind to cinders. All that I am, was, or could be... gone on the artificial wind of the ship's air circulatometer. But for a single cast of the dice, one lone side might favor me."

"Probably more like the double-zero on a roulette wheel. No offense."

"None taken. It's a fool's gambit, and explaining to someone without Mordecai's overbearing presence before me makes that so much easier to see."

"Told ya. I'm a great sounding board for decisions." Without so much as considering that she might have taken precisely the quantities she'd intended to eat, Carl stole one of her breadsticks and bit into it. He wagged the remainder. "Don't be one of the people who let that fact slip their mind."

"I can scarcely imagine another classification."

Carl chuckled. "Just leave Mort to me. Maybe I can't get him to storm Mars to look for Eric... Maybe I *can*. Won't know till I try."

There was bravado, and then there was foolishness. "You really oughtn't. Eric's beaten around the bush so much there's a walking path, but that friend of yours, in his stolen body and with his darkest of dark magic tomes, is more than he appears. Well more. You shouldn't risk his ire."

"Eric's hinted at stories he wasn't around to hear. I was *in* those stories. Mort was in *my* crew, not the other way around. And I've known him since your mother was probably your age."

This was the most infuriating human she'd ever met. Simply avoiding him or growing cross was out of the question. Cutting him out of her life was akin to trimming unwanted hair —he would just come back. He was always wrong but never seemed so. He was always right but never the proper way. He was either a sage who spoke like a fool, the galaxy's biggest liar, or—most vexingly—both at once.

And she took the bait because she *wanted* it, not because he dangled it so expertly.

"I've lost count of the times you've hinted at an acquaintance with my mother before me. How well did you know her? Were you one of her minions at some point?"

Carl grew thoughtful—amateur stage performer thoughtful, so blatant even the cheap seats would know he was pondering. "First off, no. Never worked for her. But I did strategically lose a planet to her in a poker game. Well, I had to win one, first, and lose another—it was a little convoluted, now that I'm trying to explain it all. But she had her business all up in New Garrelon's, and I had to figure some way to untangle the mess, and I had a planet I couldn't really afford to keep, so—"

"A planet?" That was preposterous. Eric's family never had that kind of money.

"Yeah. Whatever. Believe me or don't. But you asked the question. Oh, and there was that time she held Harmony's mom hostage to get my people to run the Rucker Syndicate off her turf."

"Which mother? The starlet or the politician?"

"Oh, I'll leave that to your imagination. But you know when you ship a kid off to summer camp, and they don't want to go, but when you pick them up, it's hard getting them back into the ship?"

Charlotte felt her cheeks flush. "I rescind my request for the details of your dealings with the admiral. Likewise, I absolve you of any duty to intercede with Wizard Mordecai. You don't know whom you've been dealing with all this time."

Carl looked her right in the eye. For a fraction of a second, she peeked. It was all she could do to blink in time not to get swallowed into a mirror maze of fractured psyche from which she wasn't sure she'd ever escape.

"Trust me. I do. I REALLY do."

———

A warm breeze wafted in, bearing the usual hum of insects. The humidity of Poltid's major population center had never been the planet's brightest selling point. But Esper had grown accustomed to the little annoyances, and a simple charm kept her free from mosquito bites.

Her hammock swayed. While she could have turned and watched Autumn and Grace playing some competitive puzzle game on the holovid, she had the latest Lurien Garry novel on her datapad. *Windswept* wasn't the author's best work, but Esper was fifteen books deep in the series and felt she owed herself a conclusion.

Just as she was getting to a particularly juicy scene—and feeling a slight creeping embarrassment that two of her adult daughters were just meters away—an alert popped in, overlaying the text.

While Esper had grown accustomed to letting someone else field comms from Tiffany, this wasn't from her usual ID. The alert identified the person awaiting her connection as Earth Government Acting Dictator Tiffany Bell.

Esper huffed and sat up. There was blowing off an irritating old friend, and there was blowing off the woman charged with whipping Earth back into shape following a multi-year brush with monarchy. Esper was only able to justify one of the two.

Checking her reflection, she smoothed out a case of Hammock Hair and hit Accept.

"Wizard Esper," Tiffany greeted her. It took a moment for

Esper to even recognize her former apprentice. She wore a high-collared robe, azure silk with gold embroidery. Gone were the crystalline glasses she didn't need for her vision and the ponytail she wore because it was easy. Someone had spent a good long while on elaborate braids, weaving them around a tiara that matched both the robe and the earrings that accompanied it. Gold eye shadow was, perhaps, an ostentation too far. "I've got news you may be interested in."

"The new job came with quite the fashion upgrade," Esper replied, failing to suppress a smirk.

"Fuck off. I'm still me. The outfit dates back a few centuries farther than I think anyone was happy about; the last time a Convocation wizard of the female persuasion got put in charge of government. And you pull the 'ancient imperial concubine wore it better' bullshit on me, I'm rescinding your senate seat."

Esper blinked. "My what?"

Autumn couldn't help herself. "Her what?" In the background, the sounds from the game had ceased.

"Something about a senate seat for Mom?" Grace declared.

"*What was that?*" Karen called out from the yoga room.

"Mom's in the senate, I think," Autumn bellowed back.

"Am I?" Esper asked the costumed face on her datapad.

"If you can keep your focus on the comm long enough to accept, yeah," Tiffany shot back. "Look, there's a million meetings on my schedule, and not every newly appointed senator gets a comm from the dictator. You won't have a vote that counts until Mars comes back to the fold, but in the interim, you'll be their non-voting, ceremonial senator. But you can sit on committees and have floor-speech privileges, plus a good parking spot if you decide to forgo a chauffeur and fly your own hover to work."

That would be the day. Emergencies and border colony joyrides were one thing, but Esper wasn't about to fly in Earth airspace on a daily commute. Then again, in everything she'd just heard, that was the least of her troubles.

"Everyone's going to hate me. I'm already persona non grata on Earth and Mars."

"Probably," Tiffany agreed. "But a majority of Martian voters picked you not that long ago. I sold that logic to the powers that be, and it's a done deal."

Autumn horned in on the conversation, crowding into view of the datapad's camera. "But I thought *you* were the powers that be, now?"

"See? Smart kid. Always been my favorite. I say you're a senator. Get here by Monday to get sworn in. The press release went out over the science blasts like half an hour ago, so people will hate you even *more* if you try to back out."

"Tiff, I don't know..."

"Your Earth-based assets are unfrozen. You're pardoned of anything even remotely a crime. If anyone planetside gives you shit, pass me a name and I'll have them burnt at the stake. That's not even a figure of speech. I had them set up the stake and everything. My conflagrating finger's itching to try it out. So quit whining and waffling and get to Earth to represent your fucking people."

The comm ended abruptly before Esper could formally accept.

"I can't tell if Aunt Tiffany is more of a bitch or less since becoming dictator," Grace observed.

"Less," Autumn declared emphatically. "I think she's starting to mellow out a little."

Karen entered barefoot, in leggings and a crop top, toweling off. A pair of headphones hung around her neck like a collar. "What was that? Was Tiffany on the comm?"

"Mom's been appointed senator-in-exile from Mars," Grace informed her.

"Really? You going to accept?"

Esper flushed. "I... well, I wasn't given a chance to refuse."

"Good." Karen swatted Esper playfully on the backside as she headed for the fridge and one of the overly sweet recuperative drinks Poltid produced locally. "Saves me the trouble of talking you into it."

That afternoon, Esper sat at a sweltering depot on the outskirts of town, waiting for the shuttle that would deliver her to a Nebula Interplanetary starliner bound for Earth. Alone. She'd said her goodbyes and left word with Earth that her family would follow her in good time—not uprooting everyone on an hour's notice for the last transport that could make the journey felt only fair.

Her security detail, more an honor than real protection, given that no one was foolish enough to try getting to her here in the first place, lingered at a respectful distance. She'd miss Bonbra and Alakuu, but she wouldn't miss the constant feeling that she *needed* protecting. Then again, despite Tiffany's threats to anyone who might trouble her, Esper would never *not* be a target the rest of her life.

The ground shook. Even softening his footsteps, it was impossible to miss one of the giant klemekoo approaching.

"You weren't going to say goodbye?" Kubu asked.

She turned and smiled up at him. "There wasn't time to make it to your house and back here in the little time they left me."

"There's always time. I would make them wait."

"Care to join me?" Esper inquired. "You've got diplomatic status. They can't refuse."

Kubu shook his big head. "No. Poltid needs me. I'd enjoy going but not cleaning up the mess when I got back. Things always find new ways to go wrong without me."

"Mind sitting with me while I wait for the shuttle, then?"

The pair waited in silence. Esper leaned against Kubu's flank, comforted by the furnace warmth and familiar scent of him. All too soon, the promised shuttle came to whisk Esper back into the spotlight.

Being Skogul Rasmussen sucked. Apparently, killing a suspect wanted for questioning in a massive assassination plot hadn't been the right move. Additional wizards had been sent. The whole bunker had been locked inside a web of wards that Eric couldn't even see out of.

Also, the guy couldn't eat peanut butter, his fingers hurt when he gripped a fork or spoon, and—in a more recent revelation—snored badly enough to wake himself from a sound sleep. That was going to wreak havoc in the Village of Eternity if Eric didn't fix things.

Not that he could just hop into his old body. Not only was it dead, the new wizards had been poking, prodding, and ritualling at it constantly ever since arriving.

Solutions were growing increasingly hard to come by.

One upside was that Wizard Skogul wasn't allowed at the briefings.

Eric would have traded his wave after wave of interrogations for a stale bagel and sciencey coffee over with the admirals and generals.

Worst of all, the gaggle of wizards now inhabiting the bunker had so thoroughly squelched all magic that he couldn't even warm his tea.

"Tell me again. Whom did you speak to the morning of the 20th?" The inquisitor du jour was Edward Belanger, Order of Ptah. He'd introduced the shackles that locked Eric's left wrist to the chair. Luckily, Eric could still drink tepid insta-brew tea with his right.

"I've been over this," Eric explained. The actual Wizard Skogul had been more than accommodating once informed that his choices were cooperation or nigh-eternal boredom. "I woke up at my usual 5:30 in the morning. Soaked in the hot tub until 6:03. I received half a grapefruit and a chai latte from my cook, whose name and place of residence you have in your files, and a brief, unsatisfactory sexual favor from my assistant, who is likewise known to you."

Eric had been instructed to describe the interactions exactly thusly, and he still wasn't quite sure what had transpired with the assistant.

"After that, I reported to work. I spoke to Marina in Accounting about my travel reimbursements and exchanged a perfunctory 'good morning' with Wizard Loretta. A liaison named Javier—though I only have his name tag to verify that—conveyed that I was being summoned to this very inquisition assignment."

"What about people you met incidentally? On the street. In your apartment building. Anyone."

Deep down, Eric knew that the repetition of similar of even duplicate questions was meant to break down the resolve of the one being interrogated. He was exhausted on behalf of the poor sap who thought Eric would break first.

He recounted Wizard Skogul's tales from his excellent memory. Every neighbor the man ignored. Every patron in the coffee shop beneath his building. Every pedestrian on the street along his walk to the office.

Eventually, after taking two meals and pissing into a bottle —to the horror of his captors, when they accidentally walked in on him—Eric was eventually locked into a closet where they'd stowed an extra cot.

His back ached, and all he'd done all day with it was sit.

How many years would it be before Eric's own body started hurting for no good reason, just for the simple act of existing?

Zero, he realized to his dismay. This *was* his body now. It was the loaner pair of flip-flops the civic pool provided when your locker gets robbed during a swim because you don't believe in padlocks. Sure, it got the job done, but it didn't feel right and there was both a weird smell and sticky feel to it. Someone else had used this body, and Eric couldn't know with any certainty for what.

He realized he could have asked but decided on ignorance instead.

None of that helped him fall asleep. Far from it.

The universe had shrunk to the size of a small, heavily armed motel, and Charlotte wasn't in it with him.

Eventually, simply because Wizard Skogul's body lacked the fortitude to continue on indefinitely, Eric fell asleep.

―――

Poofing into existence in the Village of Eternity came as an immeasurable relief. The Hills of Memory looped and spun as Eric pretended he knew how to do cartwheels but rotated the world instead. Nothing hurt here—except his heart. That annoying addendum to an otherwise pleasant realization soured the rest.

He missed Charlotte. He missed Jessie. He missed Uom'pe and Chinochin and Grosstet. He missed Xrista. He missed Trebla. He missed Mort and Sparta and Dad and Eric. And Eric was decidedly *unused* to missing Eric. Eric had been Eric's constant companion since before he knew his own name. As much as he insisted that the mind was the person and that everyone in the Village of Eternity was just short of a body to live in, he was now experiencing newfound empathy for the bodyless.

Mort would be the one to talk to. He'd done this before. Maybe he knew some tricks.

But Mort wasn't here.

Charlotte wasn't either, and for reasons Eric couldn't explain, that felt more important, even though she wasn't liable to be much help escaping this Martian gulag.

When Eric grew bored of cartwheels, he poofed into the library, where Uriela didn't hide how cross she still was with him.

"How fares the phlegmy carcass you've stranded us in?"

"I'm *really* sorry about that," Eric told the village caretaker.

Uriela tented her fingers as she rested her elbows on her desk. Eric got the distinct impression of not being the one in charge here. "Pause to consider that your apologies are meaningless without actions to back them. I have no interest, personal or professional, in you feeling badly about our situation. What I want is some kind of reassurance that you're fixing... well, *anything*."

Eric sighed. "I'm a little dry on ideas. I know. Not my usual problem. But I'm feeling un-Eric-like in this body."

"We are trapped in a Martian military bunker. We are under suspicion of, at the very least, dereliction of duty, if not treason, for your cover story. We are lodged in a prematurely decrepit body with a host of ailments that could likely be dealt with by either science *or* magic if we could get access to our friends outside. What here sounds like it should be our priority?"

"But I've—"

"We've," Uriela snapped. "Stop thinking in the first person singular. We're in this together. You're more than a singular being."

"I know. I know... I'm responsible for all the minds that live here in the Village."

"To hell with *them*! I'm talking about *us*!"

Eric smirked. "You're one of 'them,' too, you know."

Uriela's deadpan glare gave him pause.

"You... you *are* one of them. Right?"

The library vanished. The desk vanished. Uriela and Eric stood on a rounded green hilltop. It lacked the checkerboard mowing pattern and the floating objects in the sky. This was the origin point of the Village of Eternity, Eric's very first attempt to conjure a world of his own.

"What warning did you get about this place?" Uriela demanded sternly. "When you created it. Who stood here, and what did they tell you?"

Memories swirled. Suddenly, Uncle Enzio appeared. He melted into Mordecai The Brown before their eyes. The apparition wasn't looking at Eric; he was looking at a shade of Eric that was standing there oblivious to both the present Eric and Uriela.

"*Now, I can't say for certain, since you didn't read the book itself. But there's a chance you'll still fall prey to the book's little ploys.*"

"*Like what?*" the shade of Eric asked.

"*The book searches the recesses of your mind, scrapes together an avatar from the pieces. It'll seek to control you. To get you to do its bidding. Just remember, you're the one in charge. You can destroy it, imprison it, or simply ignore it. But the key is identifying it.*"

The shade of Eric cocked his head, and present Eric found himself matching the pose. "*How do I do that?*"

"*It'll be a dark mirror of yourself. Everything you're not, but still you. It may be hostile, obsequious, terrifying, or reassuring. But it will try to force you to obey or give up control. Just don't.*"

You'll be fine. Besides, the way I taught you, I don't think it'll happen. Just being cautious."

The apparitions vanished.

Uriela cocked her head just as Eric had done. "So?"

Eric shrugged. "I never did see that dark mirror version of me. Unless... You're not going to tell me it was Snow and Slater or anything. Mort didn't think I'd get one mirror Eric, let alone two."

"It's me."

"Huh?"

"IT'S. ME! Merlin's lunchbox, if I didn't live in your brain, I'd question its existence. I'm the dark mirror."

Eric laughed uneasily. With a wave of his hand, he sent them back to Uriela's library with her behind the desk. "Good one."

She immediately got up and circled around to Eric's side, getting right up in his face. "Look at me."

"We're nothing alike."

"No. In fact, one could say we're as different as two people could get. You, an absent-minded dreamer of a young man, indecisive, awkward, pale as a spacer, always thinking about anything but what's right in front of him."

Eric gulped. "And you're..."

"A grounded and confident older woman (young as I appear), patient and meticulous, comfortable around people I've never met. Dark-skinned. Immaculately kempt. I keep track of every detail, enforce every rule."

"I don't understand..."

"Yes, you do. Or I wouldn't."

"But you don't try to control me."

Uriela seethed in frustration. "What do you think I'm attempting? Right. Now? You need to get us out of this mess, and you're running out of time."

"Time..."

"NO!" Uriela snapped. "No time loops. You didn't start one. We can't reset and try this again. Take the night to recuperate. Tomorrow, take the first wizard you come across and switch bodies. Anything must be better than this sickly slob. Wizard Airene, if you can manage it."

"Which was she?"

"The one with the honey-blonde hair. Probably ten years older than she looks, but just proof that she cares about maintaining herself. Wouldn't mind a stint in that flesh, if we can't get our own back. Charlotte could get used to it."

Eric recoiled. "I can't go back to Charlotte as someone else!"

"Kid, it's the only option at this point. Just pick something in good shape and pleasant to look at."

"But... she's a person! I can't just... kick her out of her body."

Uriela slouched back into her chair, the first time Eric could ever recall seeing her look lazy. "Do you want the latest census numbers? You most certainly can, and you most certainly *have*. It might be harder than usual to make contact, with the suppression runes around the bunker, but you'll manage. And with each wizard you can trap here, the defenses will weaken. Take out enough, and we can walk out and hitchhike back to the *Arete*. How's *that* for a plan?"

Eric backed away. "That's... monstrous. If I wanted to kill everyone, I could have just couped. We had one all lined up and everything. The Earth people were supposed to get away. I was supposed to sneak out in the chaos. I... no. I can't. I need to find a way to *undo* this whole mess."

"Eric..."

He continued his retreat. "No."

"Eric, it's time to be practical."

"NO!"

"ERIC!"

He was gone.

Uriela was gone.

Eric stood atop a mountain peak crusted in ice and snow as bone-chilling winds blasted past without so much as rustling the fabric of his robes. From his vantage, a planet stretched out to the horizon on all sides. When he unfocused his eyes, more planets appeared just like it. Exact copies. A flipbook of time unspooling, each world a tick of a clock offset from the next. The duplicates raced off behind him, a time-lapse of the planet's orbit.

A moment later, from around the sun, the duplicates from a year back caught up with him. Imprecision caused a blur as transparent afterimages overlapped.

Around.

Around.

Around the afterimages raced.

But Eric was only looking for a spot to anchor. He judged by feel.

In the other direction, tick by tick, more planets zoomed off ahead of him. The future.

Around.

Around.

Around the premonitions streaked.

Faster.

Faster.

In both directions, the distinct ghostly worlds became indistinguishable, melting into a continuous stream, glowing with possibility. Radiating temporal power.

With a snap of his fingers, Eric stopped the procession.

He relocated to a jungle where cities will-have-once stood.

Ferns with leaves like mattresses towered over him. The ground shook with reptilian footsteps.

A roar.

Dinosaurs.

Eric grinned. Not what he was looking for, but a promising sign that he could get time to loop from the far end. At least in the Village of Eternity. At least for now.

He just needed to practice his aim.

⌑

Datawork.

Officers had always joked about it. One of the perks of special forces was that, most of the time, someone who didn't like washing other people's blood out of their hair ended up doing it for you. Team effort. Filling a role. Jessie didn't *mind* the data-pushers so long as they didn't try to tell her how to do her job or deny requisitions for ammo and equipment.

Now, it was her job to oversee everything. Charlotte had been taking more personal time lately, and the datawork didn't mysteriously disappear without her acting as the mystery.

Makket wanted to build a city? Perfect. But that involved effectively having to create the concept of building permits. Because the last thing Jessie was going to allow was unlimited, unsupervised modifications to parts of the ship she'd never see.

The 400th complaint about the food? Jessie had taken her newfound status as "not an outlaw at the moment" and placed an ad. 10,972 would-be chefs from around the galaxy had applied for the position. Even stating up front that it was unpaid, demanding, and potentially dangerous, she'd never get through all the applications before the crew starved or revolted.

Medic Daschel's reports were a minor blessing. She had two duties that Jessie received updates regarding. First was the overflow from Charlotte's caseload. She reported the fact of a counseling session taking place, the participant, and a quick confirmation that they were not deemed a threat to themselves or others. Second, and the reason Jessie checked Britney's reports promptly, were the latest flat-snaps of Blessica.

Jessie dearly hoped the name grew on her because she lacked the heart to suggest Harmony change it.

Every snap looked about the same. Squishy pink little face. Cocoon of fluffy-soft baby blanket. One in every six or so, her eyes were open.

While Jessie was getting misty-eyed about the tiny miracle that had happened aboard her ship, the door chime rang.

After a quick wipe of the back of her hand across her eyes, she called out. "Come on in."

Aunt Jamie entered, with Aunt Sofia following close behind. "Got a minute?"

"To what do I owe the pleasure?"

Sofia shrugged. "Beats me. She said she didn't want to say it twice."

Aunt Jamie looked her wife in the eye. "I think the time's finally come."

"You're leaving me for a wall of haathee tentacles?" Sofia deadpanned.

"Retirement."

Sofia chuckled reflexively before catching herself. "Wait. I was just joking, but..."

"I'm not," Jamie confirmed.

Jessie wasn't quite sure of the appropriate reaction here. Dad was semi-retired from drinking beer and playing backup guitar a couple nights a week, and he was eight years younger. Certainly, it was a rest well earned. But the vigilante business seemed to be Aunt Jamie's whole life. "Congratulations?"

Her aunt swallowed and nodded. "Yeah. Thanks."

"What about the *Scylla*? Aunt Sofia going to retire, too?"

"Damn right, I am!" Sofia replied without hesitation. "I've been waiting for this a long time."

"I'm a decade past burnt out. I'm falling apart faster than I can replace parts."

"Dr. Richelieu can—" Jessie tried but stopped when an authoritative hand came up to warn her off.

"I've been pushing ions my whole life. Trying to run toward something when all I'm really wanting is to run away. Sometime recent, and I can't put a finger on it, I found myself pushing when all my soul is telling me to rest."

"And me. Don't forget me," Sofia added.

"I don't know how to relax, not the way most people think of it," Jamie explained. "And what were my options? Retire like a pirate to some forlorn rock bought with illicit funds? Live like a pauper on some border colony, looking over my shoulder the rest of my days for someone I might have pissed off coming for payback?"

Jessie thought she had the answer but felt obliged to ask. There was a show being performed here, and she'd been raised to know her duty as an audience. "What changed?"

"Family. I want to get to know my little sisters. My other nephew. Don't worry; I'll stick around until Eric gets back so I can say goodbye. I want to visit my parents' graves, if I have to dig them myself and throw them in."

Jessie's smirk was only half sincere. "I only recently found out Dad's parents were still alive. They really as bad as all that?"

Without missing a beat, Aunt Jamie fixed her with a dead-eyed stare. "Your grandma didn't go find your granddad until I was about ready to start kindergarten. Not because she didn't want to, but because *my* grandparents wouldn't let her leave home before she was eighteen."

"Did... Dad know?"

"Brad's a smart kid. Maybe not datapad smart, but even he had the sense to figure that out. If he's kept you in the dark about Chuck and Becky, it's the best way he could have handled them. In all seriousness, I know where both of them are and have been talked out of putting a contract on them more than once."

"Six times," Sofia muttered.

"What about the *Scylla*? Who's next in line for command? Kinniss?"

Jamie didn't respond aloud. She locked her gaze on Jessie.

"Nah. No. No way. I've got the *Arete*. My own people need me."

Aunt Jamie approached and sat on Jessie's desk, twisting to look down at her. "So will mine. The work we've started, I'm hoping they can continue that with you. I'm thinking of putting the *Scylla* in mothballs, putting my crew to work here... if you'll have them."

Jessie blinked in shock. "What?"

"What even *are* mothballs?" Sofia mused.

Jamie had a ready answer and shifted topics while Jessie processed. "They're these chalky, crusty lumps about the size of a marshmallow, and you're not allowed to put them in your mouth. That's about all I knew about 'em."

"Seriously?" Jessie exclaimed.

"Oh, that, and they're for keeping Becky's prom dress from getting eaten by bugs."

"I mean about giving up your ship, your crew, your *mission*."

Leaning across the desk, Aunt Jamie put a hand on Jessie's shoulder. "I pass the proverbial flashlight to you. Against all odds, I crawled across the finish line still breathing. You're what I've been missing, what with us not having kids and all: an heir. Someone to carry on the family business."

"I *had* thought the Ramsey family business was off-brand musical entertainment."

"They're hard workers," Jamie continued. "They'll want to keep going. Maybe a few will follow my example and hang up their holsters. But they respect the shit out of you. Lead them."

"To where? Back into Eyndar Empire space?"

"Follow your gut. Do what feels like it needs doing. That's how I operated; they're used to it. And it's not a one-way street. They'll keep you honest. God, we're probably the only ship in the Milky Way with more psychiatrists than engineers. You step away from the 'good fight,' and someone'll check you."

Jessie addressed her other aunt. "Did they check *her*?"

Aunt Jamie answered before Sofia could get in a word. "I counted on them telling me when I was losing perspective. It's a big deal, having a lot of guns and a fast ship and no accountability. There were plenty of times the shit I saw got me angry enough to burn planets out of their orbits and space entire crews."

"You can refuse," Sofia insisted. "This is a lot to take on. I'm sure Kinniss or even Dr. Zazel could command the *Scylla* if they have to carry on without the captain."

"I don't think you're going to," Jamie stated firmly. "We've been scraping by with the firepower and limited space we've got. You've been stomping around this giant, echoing monstrosity you can't even fully staff. We're a match made in... well, Heaven probably doesn't handle arms dealing, but you get the idea.

"What do you say?"

Aunt Jamie stuck out a hand.

Knowing that drawing out a feigned deliberation wouldn't change her mind, Jessie reached out and shook it.

———

Eric strolled a field of wildflowers on a brilliant, sunny day. Shadows from giant, floating silver balls polka-dotted the landscape while "pedestrians" in hover belts flitted between them. He wasn't the only one down at ground level, but it seemed more like a place for picnics and children's ball sports than a means of transit.

Everything felt familiar. Maybe because he'd whizzed past it a thousand times already. Maybe because this was, fundamentally, still the Village of Eternity, and everything felt some degree of familiar.

His aim was improving.

Before now, his attempts at looping time to a few years ago had resulted in...

... dinosaurs.

... molten Earth.

... more dinosaurs.

... the Paleolithic Era, where a nice cave family shared their nuts and berries with him, possibly because he'd poofed out of nothing wearing "furs" from an animal they'd never seen before. If this had been an actual time loop, recent events might have begun human religion.

... dinosaurs again.

... Moscow, during the French Revolution, where the newspapers were all conveniently in English because Eric couldn't read Russian.

... and yet *more* dinosaurs. It wasn't that Eric was obsessed with the giant reptiles. He'd just underestimated how long their reign lasted until he'd whipped up a scale model of Time Itself and given the wheel a few spins.

This was his first stop in the future. He'd always put on the brakes early, like a tentative pedal-bike learner. Unlike with those wobbly wheely-mobiles, a late stop didn't result in hitting a curb and crashing face-first into some poor colonist's hydrangeas.

Had Eric somehow expected that humanity would scrape their planet clean of habitation, replacing their terrestrial civilization with one that orbited in the lower atmosphere? The answer to that appeared a definitive "yes" since he hadn't consulted any of the shades in the Village of Eternity.

What really mattered was that this wasn't anywhere near when Eric's troubles had all started.

But when *was* that, exactly?

Maybe what Eric needed was a suite of contingencies rather than a precise target. Whooshing all of history past him wasn't liable to result in a dartboard strike, let alone a bullseye.

Donning a hover-pack, Eric floated skyward to "walk" among the residents of this far-future time. He drew curious stares and a few friendly waves but tried to ignore it all and keep focused.

If Eric ended up before his own birth...

... and it was close enough that he'd live to see his "present" again...

... he could just be patient, become his own mentor at Oxford, and avert the whole time mess.

... and if it wasn't close enough to his own natural lifespan, he could take a more controlled hop ahead to make up the difference.

Hmm, now that he considered it, small, less ambitious leaps forward might be a better plan than trying to nail his ideal time in one go.

However, if Eric ended up back here again, nice as it was in this optimistic future...

... well, then he'd just have to go around another entire time.

Wait. What would happen to the Eric of the skipped timeline? Would he come to this exact spot, take this same mental journey, come up with—and botch—the same loop-de-loop plan?

Boy, that would be something. Erics would eventually overflow the timescape.

Was there such a thing as a "timescape," even? There sure would be, once a certain Utopian future acted as time-traveler fly paper with Eric Ramseys splattered all over it.

Less.

Less was more. Well, less was *less* but better.

Ease on up to the present. Quickity-quick little hops. A few years at a time. Just enough to sample the temporolocal fare, then on to the next era.

Overshooting his misadventures just *slightly* was where the complexities came in.

Ideally, he'd avert his five-year time jump. Uncle Enzio wouldn't have to go to Earth to give depositions about Eric's chronomancy. He'd never conquer Earth. Eric would probably still be dating Charlotte, though their relationship would take a wildly different course.

Eric could deal with that.

But once Eric was expelled from Oxford and the timeline both, things would get hairy.

He needed to meet up with Charlotte again, or he might never save her.

Telling Dad about Aunt Jamie and arranging a meet-up might save them both a lot of trouble.

He wouldn't make friends with Evander Days if they ended up as refugees on Phabian again.

There had to be some precaution to save Aunt Michelle's cake restaurant.

Eric's head spun with the possibilities and worries over

what consequences even minor changes might have elsewhere in the timeline.

Maybe he could stop an Earth/Mars civil war. But could he still help save all those people on Ghenlar Par'Mol? Would Harmony figure out super-secret light science from the haathee side of the galaxy and cure all the sick people she was planning to help? Would Jessie respect him as a wizard?

Eric found himself in a holotheater with a giant field that put the whole audience in the story. He watched a remake of *Mrs. Caulfield's Seven Daughters* with an entirely hairless cast. Everyone wore holographic wigs—holographs inside holos, which was silly in itself—and the twist with Cynthia and Carmen was telegraphed with the change of colored hair.

The familiar always felt unfamiliar when someone painted over the original.

This was, and always would be, the Village of Eternity. Any illusion that Eric was in the real world's future ended the moment he remembered that. Magic might not work the way he experienced it here. All of this realm was just his best guess, writ large and taken as foundational postulates to the Theory of Magic.

But the unfamiliar could feel familiar, too.

Eric brushed aside his fictional landscape, leaving himself in a blank void whose "floor" was simply a comforting force against his feet.

He perked an ear, same as if he'd heard a strange noise in the night, except this was no noise, and his imaginary ears were no help in locating it. No, this was more a feeling. Not quite déjà vu. Not quite a memory. Just beyond all his senses yet tantalizing him with a promise that he'd enjoy what he'd find.

If he followed.

Clearly, some siren's songs were traps, but others were just good clean fun. And this was the Village of Eternity. The fact that there was even a *mystery* here at all enticed him. The idea that it was a danger to him was simply inconceivable.

Setting aside his time travel escape plotting, and its potential to destroy the time-i-verse (Eric was still workshopping a proper name for all of history, future, and alternate histories and futures), Eric resolved to discover the source of the feeling.

Faintly, so faintly he thought his imagination might be imagining it, he made out what might have been the faint, distant tinkling of a bell...

... and gave chase.

⸺

The hangar of the *Arete* was as empty of stray warehouse flotsam and full of people as it had ever been since Jessica Ramsey had taken command. Without wanting to make a whole holiday and hullabaloo out of this announcement, Jessie had opted for haste in convening a full gathering of both crews. While cliques had unsurprisingly formed in the crowd, she'd made clear as she stood on the back of a grav sled looking over them all that there was no *Arete* section or *Scylla* section of the gathering.

With Aunt Jamie—a.k.a. "The Other Captain Ramsey"—at her side, at least a few of the sentients watching her must have had an inkling of the reason.

"Good evening, everyone," Jessie called out when she felt like everyone who was coming had arrived. Jamie's people had been ferried over from the *Scylla* and more or less stayed put, aside from a few washroom trips and some volunteers who helped the *Arete's* kitchen haul down a catering spread. The local crew had been less prompt and more distracted. Jessie could have missed a few ratatoret or any number of her aunt's people, but the only notable absences were her own wizards.

An issue she could deal with later, one on one.

The crowd's buzz faded slowly.

"Shut it!" Aunt Jamie barked. Instantly, the hangar fell silent. Even the *Arete* crewers didn't make a peep. How long might it be before Jessie commanded that level of respect?

There was only the future itself to tell her. "Welcome to the *Arete*, especially to those of you setting foot aboard for the first time. It's an honor and a pleasure to have you all here. To explain the reason for this joint gathering, I'm going to turn things over to Captain Jamie Ramsey."

Aunt Jamie gave a curt, professional nod before swapping places with Jessie at the back of the grav sled, two meters above the spectators. "To the crew of the *Arete*, I'd like to thank you for the hospitality and dedication you've shown me and my crew. I realize that for most of you, it was an act of faith and trust in your own captain, and her family ties with me, to go along with the insane operation we pulled off together and the subsequent cleanup of loose ends that resulted. But it's more than that, now. I can see it in your eyes. Every one of you. *Arete* and *Scylla* alike.

"There is a commonality of commitment, a resolve born not of desperation but of dedication. Too many in this galaxy view the greater evils of civilization with apathy, with hopelessness, with resignation. Not you. Everyone, at some point in their life, sees the suffering of others and asks themselves, 'what can I possibly do about it?' And you answered. Fight. Heal. Comfort. Care.

"Our fight has never been easy. It's rarely been rewarding. We chose a hard life over an empty one. The greater good over our own, personal well-being. Each and every one of us. We give all we have for as long as we can...

"And today, I confess that I've pushed past my limit. Far past it, if I'm honest."

There were grumbles in the crowd as the slower *Scylla* officers and crewmates started to catch on. This time, Aunt Jamie didn't scold, she simply pressed on.

"It's not fair to you. I'm slower than I used to be. Experienced, yes. But also, more set in my ways. I slip more often than I used to. You've had my back, and I both realize and appreciate that. I've hung on because, for all my growing shortcomings, I honestly believed I was still the best suited to lead our self-appointed crusade.

"But if I keep pushing, I'm going to get you all killed."

"We'd die gladly!" someone called out.

Jamie cracked a smile. "I know you would. That's why I can't let you all decide this. I kept going because I didn't have anyone else to carry on after me. But today, I announce both my retirement and my successor. I present you your new captain, Jessica Judith Ramsey, if you'll have her..."

There was a scattering of dutiful applause mixed in with shouts begging her not to retire. While the speech had been in English, many of the *Scylla* people had been listening on translator earpieces and called out in eyndar.

"She's mine and you can't keep her," Aunt Sofia called out, stealing momentum from the growing clamor. Though she was down at ground level, at the fore of the crowd, she turned and addressed her subordinates. "I promise you, she's not going to wither away, forgotten. I'm joining her in retirement, and I'll be damned if she's going to spend her remaining days regretting her choice of both the time and heir of her succession."

While this was all off-script now—not that there had been much of a script to begin with—Jessie felt the time was right to step in.

"The *Arete* was christened on the idea of excellence. We

weren't here because we were the best, we became better for being here. Together. As a herd. As the lone haathee vessel within a thousand star systems, we've met our foes with superior technology but also with greater dedication, purer intentions, and firmer resolve. We stumbled into the *Scylla* and Captain Jamie Ramsey because we saw the same evil. And maybe because of my upbringing, somehow, or something in my Ramsey blood, we came up with the same solution, which was to roll up our sleeves and fucking DO SOMETHING about it.

"I'm not one to sit idly. I'm not one to shy from a fight. And there *are* still fights out there. I'm not sure what I'd do if there weren't, and for better or worse, the galaxy we live in doesn't seem ready to run out any time soon.

"And while the *Scylla* is a fine ship, the *Arete* is better equipped not only to meet these fights head-on but frankly to fit the number of fighters I hope to bring against every threat we can find. Aunt Jamie said that I was her successor, but that's just handing over the keys to a starship. The decision to join the *Arete* as crew will be up to each and every one of you individually. You don't need to convince me; serving with Captain Ramsey is all the resume any of you will ever need. You just have to convince yourselves that this is still your war and that you want to join us to fight it.

"Once I have everyone's answers, I'll work out a new command chart and duty assignments. Our missions will expand to the limits of our capabilities, whatever they may be. I have matters to attend to with the operation of the ship. For follow-up inquiries, please address the elephant in the room."

Jessie swept a hand to Grosstet, standing off to the grav sled's side and in danger of bonking his head as she landed to disembark.

The crowd swarmed. Handshakes and hugs for both

retirees as well as a few xeno-cultural farewell gestures Jessie wasn't familiar with. Questions assailed her, but she promised that she'd get everything sorted out and that Grosstet was the go-to in the meantime.

Stragglers trailed in her wake all the way to the lift, nagging like journalists after a political scandal.

Jessie managed to board the lift alone.

Slumping against the wall, she wondered what manner of excuses she was willing to accept from Mort, Sparta, and most especially Commander Wizard Charlotte Webber for failing to show up for the occasion.

▭

"Place" was a nebulous concept in Eric's head. Actually, Eric's head wasn't much of a place anymore at all. Whether the Village of Eternity had remained in his old head, been relocated to Wizard Skogul's, or—and this was a new theory entirely—existed somewhere else altogether, sub-places inside it didn't follow any rules of geonomy, cartonomy, or astronomy.

Despite all that, Eric knew he was on the trail.

From incoherent nebulae of chaos to barren prairies. From a theme-park world he'd never gotten around to scrapping to the Hills of Memory via Uriela's library. From a trackless pink ocean to a series of airborne islands made of chocolate.

He tracked the sound.

Whether it grew louder or not, he felt as if the journey was bringing him closer to a destination.

Really, all else aside, that feeling was what truly mattered.

One landscape to the next, from familiar worlds to the abandoned or never finished, to ones he had no inkling about at all.

Eric now found himself on a medieval city street.

Whitewashed facades and Tudor architecture. Cobblestones and carriages. It only took him two intersections worth of pedestrian exploration to upgrade his assessment to Earth Renaissance European.

He had, on occasion, allowed some of his elder residents to play around with a world, here or there. Powerful terramancers and wizards within the framework of the Village of Eternity, inside a limited scope, they had nearly the powers he'd delegated to Uriela.

... which felt a lot less like a benign act of trust than it had not long ago.

But this world was on another level compared to even his own best handiwork.

The cobbles were uneven. Carriage doors were scuffed smooth at the handles from extensive use. Workers cleaned lamps of their candle soot—a detail he'd never considered. Handcart vendors hawked fish and flowers and newspapers that looked printed from either block carvings or a primitive movable press—the last wizard-acknowledged invention of the pre-scientific age.

Every person was different, unique in ways Eric hadn't the patience to replicate. His phantasms were so re-used and re-trained that he'd go years into a new world's existence recognizing them from previous roles, like familiar actors in a new holovid. And actors Eric had a habit of duplicating.

Not here.

This was someone else's handiwork.

He followed the sound, distracted by his previous mystery. It grew loud enough now that he felt like his chase neared an end.

"Ey, guv'na, fancy a charity read?" The young newsboy had a hand bell, the sort one might lift from a bedside table to summon a servant with tea, and he rang it as part of his advertising pitch.

Eric accepted the metaphor as any good dreamer might. The front page was a poem, its headline a title...

Van Winkle

I met a traveler from a recent time,

Who said—"I knew you once and shall again.

Stand on mountain peaks with me and rhyme,

A lifetime's loop, played on refrain."

The corner of Eric's lip curled in a smile.

Flipping the newspaper this way and that and turning pages, the remainder seemed unremarkable in its mundanity yet fascinating in minutiae of this land of fable. No other clues seemed to present themselves.

He heard the bell once more.

Eric handed the newspaper to a passerby who muttered grateful confusion in return.

Streets wended past him in a muddle.

Outside a public house, two chalkboards proclaimed the daily offerings to one side, and to the other, another hint.

The bell rang, or so he thought, then realized it had been the clinking of glassware.

You Could Not Stop

Because you could not stop for Death,

I stopped for him instead.

If you would draw another breath,

Come back and find our bed.

What an odd sentiment for what was little more than an old-timey bar. Dad had played gigs at some pretentious places over the years, but Eric had never noticed any with macabre poetry scratched out in chalk with excellent penmanship outside.

After a brief exchange of rather unpleasant pleasantries

with the rough clientele of the public house, Eric decided that he'd been wrong about coming here.

The bell jingled.

Wandering with his head up and his eyes open, Eric paid less attention to the sound, allowing ears and feet to communicate directly as he took in more of his surroundings.

He'd been here before, but it had been a long, *long* time. A sizable chunk of Eric's waking life. A longer span by ages and eras when it came to the Village of Eternity.

Because this wasn't the Village of Eternity at all...

Unless he'd reproduced a copy somehow (and Eric acknowledged that he just might have done so), this was Mortania.

Only Mort put this much effort and attention into a single world. His phantasms had birthdays and got hangnails and had motives and goals and errands to run. The worlds of the Village of Eternity ran on mutual imagination. Eric and his mental guests were house tinters; Mort reminded Eric of one of those hobbyists who used magnifying glasses to paint model soldiers down to the uniform buttons.

But the bell still called to him.

Eric had to know.

He followed an ice vendor's cart for a while. He threw coins conjured from air into the hat of a violinist playing at an intersection.

The coins rang as they struck, but the sound wasn't quite right. There was a hum of dissonance, a perceptible beat just like Dad tuning a guitar by ear, one string resonating with the next.

Shaking his head, Eric pressed onward.

Coins splashed into a fountain, clinking delicately off the weatherbeaten stonework. At the fountain's base, a plaque.

Two cobbled roads in a city stood,

Sorry. You cannot travel both.
Not a question if you should
A matter solely of a "could,"
A breaking or a keeping of an oath.
Sometimes life just isn't fair,
One must do what it takes,
To stave off one's own deep despair,
Resolve oneself to leave things there,
Forgive yourself and leave behind mistakes.

"This is possibly the most judgmental fountain I've ever met." He scowled a moment. "Top three, at any rate." He dropped a handful of his own coinage, listening intently. "No still not right."

Whatever city this place might have been based upon, Eric hadn't been in Mortania recently enough to remember its layout. Here and there he caught sight of a grand castle rising at the center of the city, but never did his wild goose ever lead him that way in its flight.

Bakeries and silversmiths. Cobblers and candle-makers.

Then, Eric pulled up short.

A shop that made bells.

Thousands of little jingles rang out, delighting the ears in a cacophony that held within it a symphony of little songs.

However, a single jingle caught his ear before he entered the shop.

The next storefront over, a bookshop door opened and shut, and there rang the *true* bell. The one he'd been seeking since leaving behind his time experiments.

On the shop windows, handwritten in grease paint...

Shopkeeper

Once upon a lifetime dreary, while I worked at magic teary,

Over on a debauched and misery-laden ship.

While I toiled and learned commanding, 'neath my mother, all-demanding,

Till my spirit was not standing, standing not for one more whip.

"Tis the final straw," I swore. "Standing up, I gave a quip."

"Eric, get your ass inside this door!"

The handwriting on the final line was totally different, enough to shock Eric into immediately complying with the poem's command.

He pushed through the door.

The little bell jingled.

An antique bookshop snuggled around him, cozy and smelling of ancient paper and leather and candle wax. Mort sat upon the clerk's counter, looking like the *old* Mort who ruled the dreamscape instead of like Hadrian.

But Eric's eyes immediately found Charlotte, clad in a black cardigan and skirt with knee-high boots and spectacles on a little chain, hair pulled up into a bun.

She smiled to greet him.

━━━

While her official *Arete* uniform in medical teal was, for a certain definition, appropriate attire, Dr. Harmony Richelieu knew that this was neither the time nor the place. These corporate types used to fill her day planner from 9 a.m. to 6 p.m. Monday through Friday. While occasional eccentricities were forgivable in a nepotism vice president, today she opted for a light gray business suit with a white lab coat over it, forgoing her data goggles in favor of a full, Sol-approved cosmo tint and freshly whitened smile.

On the screen in her office, a legal office conference table gleamed, surrounded by talent that was charging her a combined eighteen thousand terras an hour. In the background, the cityscape of Tokyo Prime was no illusion or fake.

Addison Takahara provided a meeting summary as the others quietly tapped final thoughts into datapads and gathered their coffee mugs. "That's it, then. The *Barton* will be registered to Harmony-Tech Incorporated by end of business today."

A little fluttering in her belly crept up and presented itself as a reserved smile. "Thank you. Thank you all. I know this has been sudden, but given the current state of things here on the *Arete*..."

"Understood, Madam President," Addison declared.

"One last item. Any potential for legal actions coming out of Harmony Bay?"

Her lead corporate attorney's ice didn't crack for an instant. "We're in the enviable position of a no-lose scenario. Harmony Bay was officially planetized by the Martian Military Government. As such, they have no standing in Earth courts to file any legal action. And with your political cover, you are essentially free to take anything you like from your mother's company until such time as a treaty ends hostilities. As a minority shareholder in Harmony-Tech, I wouldn't be averse to commandeering any corporate assets you might be able to safely access."

Harmony couldn't help a snicker. "Something to be said for the Ministry of Figuring Out How to Do What the Dictator Ordered."

"May it last exactly as long as it takes to get our production and manufacturing in place and not a second longer," Addison agreed. Despite her deadpan delivery, a few of the lawyers on the far end chuckled. Harmony as well.

"Excellent. I'll look into that. Richelieu out."

She shut off the comm panel and felt a tidal wave of relief hit her.

A six-month commitment to the *Arete* had stretched over a year as the haathee embassy ship became her asylum from treason charges. Now, the winds had shifted.

Asset seizure worked both ways, thanks to Dictator Tiffany Bell's offhanded declaration of "sure, let her take whatever the fuck she wants" when Harmony had asked about official status for the *Barton*. Frantic interim government bureaucrats had to scramble to turn that edict into actionable policy. An even more frantic rush to assemble a legal team to incorporate an ownership group, not only for the *Barton* but for the Milky Way's soon-to-be sole source for Harmony-Tech Multipurpose Medical Nano-drones.

Once they had a marketing department, someone was sure to come up with a catchy name.

For now, Harmony's Earth-based bank accounts had been enough to pay for the basics. She still owned ninety-two percent of the newborn future megacorp's stock, issued just two hours earlier and distributed to her lead attorney and a few key government allies to kick the process into orbit.

Floating on air, she hurried across to her quarters, shedding the lab coat and the jacket of her suit at the door.

"It's done!"

Xrista rushed over and hugged her. "Does that mean we can go back home?"

Home...

What *was* home anymore?

"Home is wherever we're together," she answered her own question and her eldest daughter's at once.

"Nice sentiment," Britney agreed, approaching with a gentle bouncing gait as she burped little Blessica. The infant barely reacted as she passed from assistant to mother. "But where *is* our next step. The captain seems ready to ride out fighting pirates or slavers or whatever-it-is she's cooking next. Hardly seems conducive to corpo life."

"Even holding onto Harmony-Tech stock as much as I can, my personal liquid assets are enough to buy any ship or piece of real estate we set our eyes on."

Britney furrowed her brow. "Any? I always knew you were rich, but..."

"Any," Harmony confirmed. "I can afford anything on the market and convince a lot of people to sell what isn't."

"I... uh... guess around here, you being my boss and all, seemed to flatten out the social ranks a bit."

"More than a bit," Harmony admitted. "Honestly, if we'd met on Mars, you'd have gotten a nod and a handshake if you were lucky. My people kept a wall around me, shrank my world to a network of top government regulators, heads of state, award-winning scientists, and shareholders."

"Back ya go, I guess. Right? Water finding its level and all that. You were always a bit brainy for this trigger-finger lot, eh?"

It hurt to hear it like that. Harmony *had* found her place. She was scientific leader among humankind. It was hard to say she earned the CTO position at Harmony Bay, seeing as how Mom had paved her a path since before her college enrollment. She was *qualified*. But she'd been handed the position. No amount of dancing around the issue of her head start in life could make claims of hard work and diligence sound genuine.

"I didn't just have my head in the clouds, I had it up my—" Harmony recalled that Xrista was old enough to pick up on words she didn't want the girl using. "I didn't get to know a lot of new people. And yeah, it'll be hard again. Too many demands on my time. Too many shouting, shrieking, threatening voices for me not to put a buffer between them and me, and especially between them and my family."

Britney nodded somberly. "I get it."

"You're welcome to join us."

Britney scoffed. "Thanks, Doc. I know it's been... nice... while we've been here. But I'm no corpo girl."

"How does one percent of the new Harmony-Tech Incorporated preferred stock sound, if you stay on as my personal lab assistant?"

Britney laughed. "Come off it, Doc. You could hire anyone you want. Ships. Buildings. Why wouldn't the same apply to people?"

"Two percent. Final offer."

"Two percent... How much is that, even?"

Harmony thought a moment. Without her datagoggles, she had to do some math in her head. "Well, pre-planetization, the most recent market cap I saw for Harmony Bay was around 34.8 trillion marbits. I intend to put them out of business within the next ten years, so... let's call it, conservatively, somewhere around 700 billion terras." Earthling and Martian currencies were close enough on a given day that she'd readily adapt back to the old money system.

Britney was speechless.

Harmony waited, jostling Blessica as she hummed a lullaby and waited for a burp.

"Mommy, that sounds like a lot of money." Xrista had on her Thinking Face.

"It is."

"Are we... are we *rich*?"

Harmony sighed. It was hard, insulating a kid from economics when the whole galaxy knew who they were, what their parents did for a living, and the major institutions their grandparents owned. But she couldn't just come out and lie to her, either. "Yes. Very."

"Oh. OK. Can we have cake for dinner?"

"Just because we're rich doesn't mean we can eat cake whenever we like."

"No. I mean because you did a big work thing and it went great. I can have laaku food if you want, but *you* should have cake. Miss Britney, too. And you should marry her too, now that she's going to be rich."

"WHAT?"

Britney laughed, taking the girl's claim in stride. "Not sure it works like that, sweetheart."

"It does!" Xrista insisted. "Aunt Autumn always said that you had to worry about people wanting to marry you for money, but if Miss Britney is rich, too, it won't matter."

"I... I mean..." When did her daughter turn into a matchmaker? "It's rude to try to make other people get married." If it was rude when Mom got nervy about Harmony's love life, it was both rude *and* disrespectful coming from someone still losing baby teeth.

"It's not *making*. Miss Britney already does more Mom stuff than you. She reads bedtime stories, does my hair, and Blessica already loves her and she's only four."

Four days old, Xrista left off.

Harmony's and Britney's eyes met. A little nod was exchanged.

"Nobody's worried about getting married," Britney told the girl. "Right now, we're just figuring out what comes after today."

"Tomorrow," Xrista answered promptly, and quickly enough that either her wit was sharpening or she wasn't trying to be cute about it.

"And after that, another tomorrow," Harmony added. "And another. And another. Right now, we're leaving all of those for another time."

"Tomorrow?" Xrista suggested with a sly smile. OK. This

was definitely the kid learning how to take the air out of someone. Given her exposure to numerous bad influences aboard the *Arete*, she could take solace that it hadn't gotten any worse than this.

"Sure. We'll talk about where we'd like to live and where to set up Harmony-Tech corporate HQ tomorrow. Tonight, I think we can forget all that and just celebrate with cake."

━━

Grosstet had an office.

If one were of a pedantic mindset, this was a room, and it had always been his. One of the many, many chambers of the *Arete* that he hadn't handed over to anyone else in particular. But Jessie had asked little of him during her command of his ship. The occasional help on the bridge. Attending briefings. That sort of thing.

Today was the first time he'd gotten to have interviews. It was like a human holovid, and he was the interrogator.

Across the desk from him, perched on a chair atop a small flight of steps, one of Captain Jamie Ramsey's officers eyed him with awe. It was a look to which Grosstet had grown accustomed in small space.

This one, an Ensign Eebok, was plouph but spoke eyndar plus a smattering of English. Luckily, Grosstet had brushed up on the canine language and was able to communicate effectively with the newcomer.

"YES. WE HAVE A GREAT MANY UNUSED CHAMBERS ABOARD. SOME HAVE BEEN MADE INTO STORAGE. HOWEVER, THE CREW WILL HAVE TO GROW MUCH LARGER BEFORE EACH OFFICER CANNOT HAVE THEIR OWN PRIVATE QUARTERS."

The plouph bobbed his head. "Nice. Nice. Yeah. Real nice. Bunkin' with three guys. Yah? Be nice to stretch in bed without my arms up in someone else's business." He bared his fangs in what must have been an attempt at a smile.

Grosstet peered at a datapad he'd clamped to one of his tusks in convenient view. "YOUR FILE SAYS YOU HAVE MEDICAL AND SECURITY TRAINING. WHICH IS YOUR PREFERENCE?"

"I'm security. No question there. You're just starting. Gonna see a lotta med stuff. Cross-training, cap'n called it. So what if a pirate or slaver gets away. We'll keep after 'em. Whole point is rescues. Yah? Keep 'em breathin'. Keep 'em hearts beatin'. Get 'em to a real doc. Most the time, I'm muscle." He flexed an arm and patted the muscle above the elbow. Since he had more muscle in his trunk than this creature's entire body, Grosstet had to make an effort not to look egregiously unimpressed.

"VERY GOOD. I WILL LIST YOU ON THE ROSTER FOR SECURITY. YOU WILL SEEK MAKKET. HE WILL HELP FIND A LOCATION FOR YOUR NEW QUARTERS."

Next to visit, a vish kinah with tiny little datagoggles and a medical coat. This one, according to his personnel file, was Dr. Zazel. There was neither a surname nor sobriquet.

Grosstet didn't know whether the mononym was due to cultural practices or the fact that the *Scylla* was the kind of ship that didn't *have* personnel records, and a small team of officers was writing up these dossiers on their own crewmates off the cuff, as humans said.

"WELCOME, DOCTOR."

"You may address me in English, sir. I'm well versed and frankly more comfortable with it. Fits the lips better, if you catch my meaning. Plus, it's the local common tongue. I've heard the younger captain's eyndar, and I wouldn't want to be trying to have her command a vessel that way."

"ENGLISH IT IS, THEN."

"Your own command of this region's linguistics is impressive, if I may say so."

"YOU ARE ALREADY APPROVED TO JOIN THE CREW IF YOU CHOOSE. FLATTERY IS BOTH OPTIONAL AND ENTIRELY JUSTIFIED. YOU ARE JUST A DOCTOR, CORRECT? MANY OF YOUR COWORKERS HAVE MULTIPLE ROLES."

"Just... JUST, you say? Sir, I am board-certified by the Phabian Ministry of Health in emergency care, thoracic and neurosurgery, cosmetic and reconstructive surgery, immunology, parasitology, and venereology, with certificates in grief counseling, post-traumatic stress, dissociative trauma disorders, and workplace conflict resolution."

"I HAVE TINY ROBOTS IN MY BLOOD."

"Yes. I'm aware that your outgoing Chief Medical Officer is intent on rendering much of my profession obsolete. In the meantime, I suspect I will be the clear choice to succeed Dr. Richelieu. My focus is on patient care, not clinical field research."

"THANK YOU, DOCTOR. I LOOK FORWARD TO YOU TAKING GOOD CARE OF THE OTHER SMALL PEOPLE ABOARD THE *ARETE*."

Grosstet skipped sending Dr. Zazel to see Makket. As soon as Harmony had informed the senior staff that she wouldn't be remaining with the combined crew, they'd decided that once she moved out, the Chief Medical Officer's suite would be ideal for whoever took over the job. Directly across from Med Bay, it eliminated the possibility of work/life balance for the person in charge of the crew's healthcare.

After that came an attractive stuunji lady by the name of

Nim Jann. She took the steps two at a time and barely fit into the chair. "Hi." Her English accent was weak, but he credited her for trying.

"GREETINGS, NIM JANN. I UNDERSTAND THAT YOU WERE RESPONSIBLE FOR CAPTAIN RAMSEY'S PERSONAL SAFETY."

"Yes." She smiled. Grosstet noted that she wrung her hands, a sign of nerves.

"YOU ARE STILL LEARNING ENGLISH?"

"Yes."

He switched. "WOULD YOU BE MORE COMFORTABLE IN YOUR OWN LANGUAGE?"

Nim Jann perked up instantly. "You speak yarbuk? Where did you learn? Nobody off the Garrelons speaks yarbuk."

"AT ONE TIME, I HAD INTENTIONS TO IMPRESS SOME CULTURAL DANCERS. IT TURNS OUT, I DID NOT NEED TO SPEAK THE LANGUAGE TO ACCOMPLISH THAT."

She narrowed her eyes at Grosstet, suspicious. "Did you just...?"

"I AM VERY IMPRESSIVE IN ALL WAYS," he assured her. Trying to maintain a semblance of professionalism, he returned to his plan for this interview. "CAPTAIN JAMIE RAMSEY WAS GROWING ELDERLY. SHE HAD MUCH NEED FOR PROTECTION. CAPTAIN JESSICA RAMSEY IS MORE INTERESTED IN SOMEONE TO SAFEGUARD THE CREW AND IMPORTANT GUESTS. IS THIS A ROLE YOU CAN LEARN?"

"Learn?" Nim Jann echoed. "Do you know how hard it is guarding a woman who refuses to take precautions, who still goes on off-ship assault missions without remembering her bones are old, and who doesn't take advice that would lower risks to herself?"

"YES," Grosstet affirmed. "MY THIRD WIFE DIED IN BATTLE. I COULD NOT CONVINCE HER OF THE DANGER SHE FACED. I WOULD HAVE FACED IT FOR HER..." He hung his head. Nim Jann's words had picked at an old scar and drawn blood.

"Well, I kept Captain Ramsey alive despite her efforts. And it will be very nice to have a ship where I can stand my full height and doorways that don't make me duck."

Grosstet took note of her size. Significantly taller and sturdier than the dancers he'd met.

It was a time of change and a flood of new friends to meet. If he did well, Grosstet's herd would grow considerably.

But the reminder of Tuunang's death only deepened his sadness that no matter how many plouph, vish kinah, and stuunji the new *Arete* crew took on, there would never be another haathee.

A day off from work caught on like wildfire. Aside from a small contingent from Logistics, without whom the *Arete* almost literally stopped functioning, and a rotation helping keep the hangar traffic back and forth to the *Scylla* humming, the rest of the crew had been relieved of duty pending a decision on just what those duties might entail and who'd be ordering them around.

With tourists and future crewmates alike wandering the vessel, a cluster of *Arete* old-timers found an out-of-the-way art exhibit with floor-level cushioned seating and camped out with booze and snacks.

The artwork was close to Earth impressionism and depicted a lot of dancing haathee and what, presumably, were some kind of nature spirits. Without understanding more of their culture, Trebla found the imagery a mixture of wondrous and threatening. At any moment, the tint could peel off the walls and come after an unwary viewer.

He had to stop smoking before watching horror holos.

"I never thought I'd end up living on a starship when I had a chance to go anywhere I wanted," Aubrey stated, sipping a margarita through a straw despite her glass being rimmed in salt. It was only 0930 hours, but who gave a shit today? "Then I saw that they were building me my own quarters in the new ratatoret city. I'm going to be living right next door to Monodex and Galapap. I've never... like... *belonged* anywhere before now."

DeAndre nodded along, then took a swig of Grosstet's home brew. "Whelp, not me. Don't get me wrong. Never felt I wasn't welcome. Just... Got me some time off the dirt to think about shit. Took it. Feelin' like time to get back to the world."

Figgy blew a cloud of cigar smoke. "You need work? I finally took a buyout from the captain. That Cavalier-class can use a couple extra employees. Wouldn't mind not having to answer questions about this ship."

"You smooth?" DeAndre asked Lorenzo.

Figgy's former—and apparently future—business partner shrugged. "Wouldn't mind a drinking buddy. Plus, how else will I ever get back the 225T you owe me from last month's poker night?"

"Security will miss you," Daphne told DeAndre.

"Weren't nothing personal," DeAndre assured her. "Thought Kinniss woulda got that gig for sure. Considered staying when I heard it was one of us. Still... man's gotta find his place."

Mindy hoisted a tankard. "Goes for a woman, too. Know mine." She leaned against Daphne, with one of the azrin's bare arms draped over her protectively. She gave the dangling hand a squeeze. "Got this brawny, flightless bird all to meself. Jess'll do the ceremony, she said. Ain't sure what tradition, though."

Daphne extended a lone claw and dragged the smooth back of it down Mindy's cheek. "She might look good with mating scars."

"Nowheres visible, luv," Mindy protested. "Might not lose me that cushy gig at Tactical, but damned if I won't lose all respect aside from on Meyang, marked up as your property."

Daphne snickered. "Well, no one would believe that you're the one who actually..." She trailed off, and if Trebla had learned anything about reading fur bristling, the azrin had just embarrassed herself. She took refuge in her mojito.

Trebla gallantly stepped in to deflect attention to himself. "Well, not that I won't be spending plenty of time in the ship's guts, but I think I'll be happy taking over as Science Officer. More equations. Fewer waste-reclaim clogs."

"I still think I'm making a mistake," Jasmine insisted. "I'm not Chief Engineer material."

Trebla took her bare foot in his lower hand. "Hey, you know this stuff better than anyone. And with Jomek retiring, it's not even close."

"Our quarters are still going to reek of ferroacoustic gel and plasma-torch exhaust," she warned him.

Learning from Daphne's mistake—and, of course, stone sober—Trebla declined to point out that the smell of that haathee power conducting gel in her hair was a turn-on. "Plenty of change on the *Arete* coming. Why switch up everything at once?"

"Every raging river needs rocks," Figgy declared.

Mindy scoffed. "Say that twice. Doc said, before she skedaddles, if me and Daph wanted, she could get us knocked up, all mutual and science-like, as if we's same species, different bits, rather than the other way 'round."

"She showed us theoretical flatpics," Daphne added.

Aubrey perked up. "Do you have them? What did your kids look like?"

"Din't keep nothing," Mindy declared with a shudder.

"They were cute," Daphne countered. "Two versions. With me as birth mother, black-furred, with normal ears but round pupils, and fingernails instead of claws. If Mindy were to carry the child—"

"Ain't happenin'."

"—then it would have been dark-skinned but white-haired, with yellow-green feline eyes and fangs in place of incisors."

"No offense, but how in the hell is that 'cute'?" DeAndre asked.

"They was Xrista's age," Mindy explained. "Nothin' ain't cute when it's that li'l."

Trebla caught an elbow in the ribs. "What'd I do?"

"I saw that look," Jasmine accused. "Don't get all misty-eyed about Doc Harmony's illegal gene-splicing hobby. She was *not pregnant*, and now there's Blessica. And did anyone *here* cough up half a dose of DNA? I know she's a newborn, but c'mon. Just look at her sister and tell me Harmony Richelieu isn't either cloning herself or splicing DNA from one of her siblings."

"Yeah, Jaz," Trebla muttered. "We all say it *behind closed doors*. But it's a hell of an accusation."

"I believes it," Mindy stated, toasting with her pint glass. "You ain't got the confidence to snip up an azrin-human hybrid if'n you ain't got the basics down."

"And there will *not* be any laaku-human babies. Got it?" For a moment, there was no one else in the chamber, just Trebla and those eyes of Jasmine's.

"Yeah. Got it."

Jasmine relaxed, slouching comfortably against him as

Trebla laced his fingers with her toes. "Good. I shot the doctor down months ago when she asked. Told her to drop it and not mention it to you, or she'd be smelling a new, different room every day from her life-support blowers."

"Anyone seen Chik-ta?" Lorenzo asked. "We were thinking of seeing if he'd join up."

Trebla shook his head. "He's packing up on the *Scylla*. Jax and Lisa were going to drop him off in League space somewhere near his homeworld before they mothball the ship for Aunt Jamie."

Daphne flattened back her ears. "You know they're going to steal it, right? The *Scylla*."

That drew chuckles from the *Arete* crewers and a dismissive wave from Trebla. "Naw. Those two? I mean, they're outlaws, sure. Mercenaries? Yeah. But have they always done right by... ... shit. Should we warn someone?"

Mindy narrowed her eyes and sipped. "Old bird musta known. Parting gift, I reckon. They'll get a few *Scylla* folks to scrape off with them. Ease the hard feelin's from the ones who don't wanna hop horses."

"Speaking of getting off the ship, have you spoken to Captain Ramsey about our honeymoon plans?" Daphne asked. And Trebla was wondering if she was airing her personal business to get Mindy to commit to an answer publicly.

"Brushed off. Sure. We can swing by. Ain't gonna happen till Eric's back in the roost. Startin' to worry 'bout that lad. Fun's fun, but deep cover work don't typically come with overtime pay if you stay extra."

Trebla felt a reassuring squeeze from Jazzy clenching her toes. "He'll be OK."

"Yeah." Trebla wished he could be so easily convinced. "Would be nice if we could get word that he was on his way back, though."

Jessie didn't know how to feel about the starship *Mobius* sliding through the hangar aperture of her *Arete*. She'd grown up on that little hunk of metal. Since she couldn't picture Mom having them buffed out, there were still probably names she didn't want to forget on the wall of her bedroom. It was a litany of transient friends from a time in her life where the only constants *were* that ship and its occupants.

It looked old.

Jessie had no doubt that the engines were up to snuff. Life support. Nav. Comms. All the basics. Enough people cared about her parents that New Garrelon orbital control wouldn't have let them offworld without a safe ride. But the tint job was older than her new Chief of Security, and the groan of the cargo ramp hydraulics set her teeth on edge.

Then, she saw Mom.

Mom was too old and Jessie too dignified and important to rush across the twenty-meter safety keep-out from the landing site and crash into a hug. But that didn't stop either of them.

"Jess... you always find new ways to worry me," Mom whispered a centimeter from her ear as they embraced.

"I'm OK. I really am."

Aunt Jamie shook her head and glanced aside at her brother. "Huggers. I'm related to a bunch of huggers."

Dad shrugged. "Came with the package."

But Mom was only the beginning of the flood. Aunt Shoni and Uncle Roddy ambled down the ramp to fuss over Trebla while his brother Dek meandered after them, clad in an expensive suit and stylish datalenses, looking like he was planning to put in an offer to buy the *Arete*.

Jessie presided over in-person introductions. More hugs. Tentative laughs. A tear or two.

Jomek and Dad had their bags packed, and Jessie and Trebla both helped carry their belongings aboard. Dad's old buddy borrowed Jean's quarters, and Jessie paused with a look to Mom before delivering his stuff to theirs.

Mom sighed. It was just the two of them at the moment. "If I divorced him every time he endangered our lives, lied to me, lost track of you kids, the legal expenses would bankrupt us both. And I'm not sure it's fair anymore to hold him accountable for Eric."

With a tight gulp, Jessie nodded and proceeded to dump her father's luggage on the floor by his and Mom's bed.

Mom followed her in. "I *do* blame you, though."

Jessie looked up. She caught the moistness in Mom's eyes. "I know."

"You're his commanding officer. You should have known better."

Jessie shook her head. "He's not like he used to be."

"I know. He comms more often than you do. Even as a wizard."

"We had—"

"You had an idea of how to rescue your father. I can tell just by looking at him that he's put on weight. The eyndar were one thing. But you couldn't have just played ball with Earth and gotten him free without putting Eric in danger?"

Jessie opened her mouth to argue without even having a clear strategy, but she didn't get a chance to start.

"And don't give me the ninety-some-odd murders as some kind of excuse. Enzio killed a lot more people than that destabilizing Earth Empire."

"He's going by Mort now."

"Good for him. I don't care. He concocted the plan that left Eric stranded on a deep cover mission on Mars." When Jessie scowled at hearing that, Mom caught on in an instant.

"Charlotte. Charlotte told me everything. She's the reason Eric remembers to comm me. Something about him appreciating having a 'real' mother. I honestly don't know that he'll ever get around to proposing to her, so I'm just skipping to considering her a daughter-in-law. And she's my informant on the *Arete* One of several, I might add. Don't think you're getting away with anything out here without me knowing about it."

"Yes, ma'am."

"Is that all you have to say for yourself?"

"I've missed you."

Stern Mom faded a touch. "I'm never so far that you can't visit."

"Maybe stay? There's a thousand kilometers of extra space around here."

"And do what? Nanny the crew? Teach fighter pilots? Your father likes playing soldier when it suits him; I'm happy leaving my uniform in a vacuum bag under the bed." When Jessie's eyes strayed, Mom nodded. "Yeah. Still down there. Still haven't broken that seal since I gave up Earth Navy for good. But it suits you. The life. Not Earth Navy, specifically. Command looks good on you."

"You're my mother."

"You think I wouldn't tell you if you needed to stop gallivanting all over the galaxy picking fights?"

OK. There was no arguing that point.

"*Hey!*" Aunt Jamie called out from the common room. "*Should we, like, clear some of this stuff out, or was the collection meant as a courtesy?*"

Jessie's face fell, her eyes shot wide. "Did Aunt Yomin not clear out her gadgets?"

Mom shrugged. "I didn't check. Don't worry about it. I don't think she'd mind."

That wasn't the point. She'd just started getting to know

Aunt Jamie and Aunt Sofia. There was such a thing as making a good impression, and the extended family wasn't helping.

Putting aside thoughts of what toys her aunts might find in their temporary quarters, Jessie corrected orbit. "You can drop off Jamie, Sofia, and Jomek, then head back. Offer stands."

Mom sighed and gave Jessie a quick hug. "Jess, somewhere out there, there's a two-bay refueling station with a pub attached that's never heard Black Sabbath played live. Small children growing up in League space think that human cultural music is digital. There are entire breweries out there whose offerings haven't been sampled directly from the tap. Who could live in a galaxy like that?"

"Not Dad," Jessie agreed sullenly.

"Now. I know some people have places to be. You, personally, are going to be ready to get Eric off Mars the second he pokes his head above ground. My passengers have lives to get back to or to start over. But first, I want to get face-to-face with that no-good, body-hopping Enzio."

That came as a shock. Jessie had ordered him to keep away from the hangar until the *Mobius* had departed. There was being mad at Dad, whom Mom had been dealing with for decades—and she was getting exactly the man she'd signed up for—and being mad at Uncle Enzio, whom she'd never especially cared for and mostly kept around because he was cheap astral travel and a good influence on Eric.

"You sure?"

"Oh, he's not getting off without me giving him a piece of my mind."

"You know he was Emperor Khosrau for a while, right?" While Mom was family, and Mort seemed unusually lenient with anyone from her old "herd," it seemed like a bad idea to intentionally poke a bear when that bear was also an amoral, soul-devouring pyromaniac.

"Exactly! How *dare* he let us hold a fucking *funeral* for him!"

"So... *not* the Eric thing?"

"Oh, I'm furious about that. But... I've tried. You know? I've tried being mad at everyone I can tie to his disappearance. I'm worried about him. But Eric... Eric's a grown man. If anyone's responsible for the way he makes decisions out on his own, it's me."

"Mooom, no." Shit. This was one of the signs Dad had always told her to look for. "You're not responsible for his—"

"Tut-tut-tut," Mom cut in, wagging a finger to warn Jessie off interrupting her rant. "I let him spend too much time around Enzio. He started thinking that magic could solve all his problems if he just got good enough at it."

"It *does* seem to have worked out for Mort."

"I needed to show him better. This is all—"

"Hey!" Dad chimed in, barging into his own bedroom without knocking. "Oh. Am I in the middle of a rant about how everything Eric does is your mom's fault and how she's failed him as a parent?"

"No." "Yes."

"Super. Amy, cool your ions. Eric's fine. Call it a gut feel. But we've got a three-month rule in this family. It's actually come up. Jamie broke the code, but that just gave us permission to grieve her. No fair picking out flowers for our middle kid when he's probably binging military-surplus-grade ice cream and cleaning the clocks of a bunch of paranoid Martian admirals at poker."

"Mort broke the code, too."

"Oh. I knew," Dad chimed in. "Wasn't my secret, so I couldn't say. But that first Khosrau speech from the coronation, I knew it was him."

As always, with Dad, it was impossible to tell whether that

was true or not. Lies about motives, facts, knowledge, that stuff was unprovable. The important thing she'd discovered was not caring. It didn't matter whether Dad knew or when. Mom hadn't. But Jessie simply didn't have enough mental energy for this fight.

"Can you go round up Mort? Mom wants a word."

"Several words," Mom clarified.

Dad grinned. "Can I stick around to watch?"

"No," Mom snapped. "I'm not letting you stand there defending him. The captain of the Oxford bowling team doesn't need *your* help answering for himself."

Rather than argue, Dad huffed a quick sigh. "Oh well. One of my guilty pleasures is seeing wizards get their robes pulled over their heads, and I can kind of see that coming."

Alone once again, Mom took the opportunity for another hug.

"You sure about leaving?"

"Jess... this is your ship. I just wanted to see you in person, yell at Enzio, and get picked up in the trunk of your haathee friend."

Sliding back her sleeve, Jessie tapped her TeleJack and opened a comm to the bridge. "Commander Grosstet, report to the hangar. My mother would like to be impressed by your physique."

"*I SHALL DELIVER MYSELF PROMPTLY AND AT MY MOST IMPRESSIVE.*"

Mom got this little schoolgirl grin. It was good to see her happy over something so stupid and simple.

North of sixty, her parents were both children at heart.

Time had flown past.

Charlotte's little bookshop made core-world bankers seem like they kept late hours. It didn't matter how fast Eric's or Mort's realms could run. The collaborative effort only worked in Charlotte's mind. She couldn't make the journey to his without direct contact, and Mort wasn't letting Eric camp out in Mortania for reasons that were both understandable and a little hurtful.

Mort didn't trust Eric.

It wasn't that Mort thought he was a bad person; Mort had never held that against anyone. It was that what Eric wanted to do, what he attempted to do, and what ended up actually happening formed a Venn diagram where the overlapping middle bit was too small for everyone's liking.

But none of that mattered now.

Eric had a plan.

As morning whisked him away though a blur of mental landscape, Eric clutched a scrap of parchment in his hand. While native to the bookshop, it survived the transit to the library in the Village of Eternity.

Uriela shared a cold glare with Eric upon his arrival.

"I don't have long. My eyes are almost open. Can I trust you, leaving this here?" He held out the parchment, rolled tight but unbound, unsealed, not even tied with a bit of ribbon.

"Eric, I'm your opposite, not your enemy," the caretaker of the Village of Eternity told him as she accepted the document.

"Yeah, but—"

"Describe me. My traits."

OK, this was a trap. Obviously. But Eric felt compelled to play along. "You're diligent, bookish, concerned with everything being just so. You take care of everything because you know if you don't, no one will. You don't mind being responsible, even if it means you have more work than everyone else. And you have power but don't abuse it."

"About *me*, personally. What do you know about *me*?"

Eric struggled to separate the woman from the job but did his best. "You're thoughtful, kind in a sort of patronizing way. You take the smallest details into account when making someone happy. You have a silly, playful side that you keep hidden because you feel like it's important that everyone see you as dignified and calm and in control. You're more concerned with making life good for everyone else than for yourself, to the point where I have to make you take a lifetime here or there for a vacation."

"Good. Now. Describe Wizard Charlotte."

"Well, she acts stuffy around other people but she's got this beautiful creative side. She rarely does anything without a plan. She's a perfectionist, but she hates that side of her and tries to push it aside. She doesn't like getting credit, but she goes out of her way to do little things to make me happy. She..." Eric was finally seeing the trap; he was standing among the wooden spikes, staring up at the hole he'd so diligently climbed into. "You're not her."

"I'm not. I'm you. And if she's got a 'dark' opposite, I imagine that it would be a free spirit with boundless energy who doesn't care how other people see her and who would indulge whims as they came and didn't take herself the least bit seriously."

"What are you saying?"

"If you can trust her, you can trust me. I *like* her. I understand her just as much as you baffle me. You're never happier than when you're with Charlotte, and I've watched the two of you cavorting through a hundred worlds, so I know it's the same for her. I bear neither of you the least ill will. I'll keep your list safe and make sure you can access it.

"Now... WAKE UP, ERIC!"

———

Eric's eyes snapped open. He was still in Wizard Skogul's body, which it was hard to argue wasn't his at this point. Stiff and sore, he grunted as he rolled and pushed himself to a seated position.

There was a plan.

Today was his escape.

There wasn't a moment to waste.

While there hadn't been long to explain in either direction, Mort had known all the Martian wizards by name, which sped up the process considerably. Eric's list had been carefully arranged based not only on relative power but on proximity within the sleeping arrangement he'd described.

The other cots in the room with Eric contained Wizard Tranqlin, Wizard Esteban, and Wizard Pete.

There was something almost quaint about a wizard named Pete, but Eric knew that his full name was Wizard Pyotr Alekseyvich IX, which explained the need for a balance to that much pretension. However, for Eric's purposes, he was Peter Target the First.

Tiptoeing over amid snores, Eric strained and struggled against an overwhelming oppression in the air. If twenty years' hard labor in a gulag could be packaged as an air freshener, the Martian bunker stank of it.

Eric didn't need much. Just a touch. Just a nudge. Just a suggestion.

Give me a few minutes free of him.

Then, just as the tapping of Eric's finger awakened him, Wizard Peter was gone.

It wasn't much, but it was a start. Peter hadn't managed a fuss before his departure, and he'd be back before long. Creeping over to Wizard Esteban, he tried again.

Get rid of him for an hour or so.

Wizard Esteban poofed.

Wizard Skogul's ragged lungs were aching with Eric's quickening breaths. He could feel the gentle drying of the sopping blanket smothering magic throughout the bunker.

Wizard Tranqlin didn't so much as flinch at Eric's touch.

See you tomorrow.

Now, Eric was alone in his shared quarters. He waited the few minutes. When Wizard Pete reappeared in a panicked daze, Eric launched him forward yet again.

Until next week.

Mort's plan had been a simple one, albeit with a grudgingly complete reliance on chronomancy. Aside from blanket protections against all arcane usage, which Eric could at least struggle against, there was no particular defense against time magic. All Eric had to do was unweave the suppressive blanket one wizard at a time, picking away at it like one loose thread at a time, starting with the easiest to corner alone and prioritizing the weakest first.

No point in trying to slice open a flat-felled seam when a simple plain seam was available to cut, weakening the fabric quicker.

It had been a surprising education in tailoring techniques that Eric hadn't been expecting as part of his escape plan. Charlotte, having grown up around costume designers and fashionistas, naturally knew all this stuff already. But it was Mort's extensive understanding of garment handicrafts that came as a shock.

Now, however, Eric had an hour or so, minus a few minutes, to really start clearing some jerk wizards out of this region of the timeline.

Eric Ramsey, Order of Chronos.

He liked the ring of it, even if it was a title given by himself.

However, he accepted Mort's premise that if at any point in the future he were to found such an order, the retroactivity of the honor would be entirely appropriate.

Out into the hallway he ventured.

Two Mars Marine Corps guards vanished without him even needing to touch them, bound for a year's exile.

However, that was possibly a mistake.

Mort had instructed him to start small, be cagey, careful. Fly below the treetops. Eric was underground. If there were trees anywhere, they'd be several basement levels above him. How could he *not* be flying underneath them?

His newfound freedom to work magic was crushed from him.

"*Raise the alarm! Unauthorized magic on the premises!*"

Darn it! Someone had noticed. It wasn't the whole "they're stronger than you, so start small" aspect that had bitten him; it was the "sneak a bunch of them out the door while the ship's still hovering" he was failing at.

They'd noticed.

Or at least, one person had. And they hadn't kept quiet about it.

In a panic, Eric's mind raced. His feet took initiative on their own.

He shut his eyes for a quick reference of the list. They opened again when he careened face-first into General Kassidy.

"The hell you doin' running around with your eyes shut?" the Martian general demanded.

"Um. Searching using my mind." It was a better lie than he'd expected to spring to mind on zero notice. Before he could jettison the general into someone else's calendar, the older, more robust soldier grabbed Eric by the upper arm and manually turned him around.

"Lockdown. Get with it. Can't have you page-turners going to pieces. Stop any magic around here."

Using his feet primarily to keep from being dragged along, Eric complied.

Hold it all steady. Nothing to cast here. Move along.

Before he knew it, Eric was in the midst of a briefing room with Supreme General Bob Randall holding court.

"... and this is going to be the last time anyone fucks this up. Maybe you're watching me on the holos and buying the nice guy act. I have the power to bust a four-star admiral to kitchen duty and send wizards off to tinker with star-drive repairs in the border colonies. You hear me?"

Eric joined an impromptu chorus and answered, "Yes, sir."

This was horrible.

So many wizards. More than yesterday, by his count. There were names he hadn't gotten yet, belonging to unfamiliar faces. His own magic was like a toddler swaddled to play in the snow, arms and legs so encased in layers of protective warm clothing that he was unable to do more than squirm and waddle.

"No one is leaving this place until we get our shit *SECURED!*"

Again, Eric's numbered among the many voices echoing, "Yes, sir."

"I can't heeeear you!"

"YES! SIR!" If volume translated directly to enthusiasm, the admirals and generals and wizards could have rivaled Grosstet just then.

Going nowhere...

Eric couldn't continue on like this. These Martians were fools, but the wrong kind. They weren't going to let him slip away unless he enacted the slippage proactively. And his attempt to do just that had resulted in a security upgrade to the bunker.

Oh...

Oh... ... ...

Eric didn't know what else to do. He'd made *such* a mess of this and after working *so* hard to do things the "right" way. His only recourse at this point was to spin the wheel and see what the next universe might have to offer as an alternative.

Let's get past the end of this timeline. Take us around again.

The other wizards in the bunker might as well have had a pillow over Eric's face for all that the universe seemed to hear him.

Maybe if he got close, he could take out one or two more, even just a minute out of the timeline, and he could work from there. Break their stranglehold. Get back to longer eviction. Create a pileup of temporal refugees a few years into the future.

Eric tried to slip sideways through the crowd.

He pushed and jostled.

"It's him! He's making a break for it!"

What? No. That wasn't it at all! If anything, Eric was all the more intent on remaining until he could make his getaway cleanly. Wizard Keemi was just on the far side of the door and next on Mort's list. Not that he could use that as an excuse.

Firm hands closed around Eric's upper arms. It was as if someone had done research and determined that to be Eric's weakness—and perhaps someone had. Or perhaps, as a scrawny nobody of a wizard, it was just that obvious a solution to any danger he posed.

"Who the fuck IS this guy?" General Bob demanded.

"Wizard Skogul Rasmussen, Order of Hypnos, General," one of the senior wizards informed their supreme leader. "He's the one who killed our only lead, supposedly by accident."

Eric needed to think of something fast. The two holding him were Mars Marines, easily ten times as strong as him. The room was half filled with wizards who, at least in aggregate, vastly overpowered him.

He needed a way out, and these people weren't even confident in his cover identity's innocence as it stood. Convincing them that he *was* actually Skogul Rasmussen, Order of Hypnos, wasn't going to gain him anything. If possible, acknowledging himself as a weakling local wizard only exacerbated the power imbalance.

What would Mort do?

Mort wouldn't have been in this predicament. Mort would have been looking for a dry cleaner to wash admiral-dust off his sweatshirt by now. Mort wasn't the role model Eric needed just now.

What would Charlotte do?

Charlotte wouldn't have been in this predicament, either. Charlotte knew she was no planet-shaking wizard and rationed her recklessness accordingly. Charlotte was a better role model, but it was too late to know better and never have come to Mars at all.

What would *Dad* do?

Dad had gotten himself into and out of so many predicaments it defied belief. Dad knew he couldn't outgun, outfight, or outsmart every foe in the galaxy, and he certainly knew he was no wizard. Dad knew that distraction, diversion, and deception ruled the day, but also that sometimes, the truth was the best lie of all.

"I'm not Skogul Rasmussen. I'm Eric Ramsey, Order of Chronos. Say goodbye to the next five years of your life!"

In the split second of shock, Eric struck.

Send everyone in the bunker five years into the future.

Oh, crap. *Wait, make that everyone except—*

But it was too late. At least partially.

Time froze. Mouths hung open, mid-exclamation of

outrage or disbelief. Limbs stopped partway through gestures of blame and accusation. One cup of coffee had been dropped and another toppled by an errant elbow on the table, but neither had finished their spill. Nor did it appear that they would.

Eric's captors had become statues; however, they still had him by the arms in meaty, oversized fists that might as well have been made of stone.

"Crap."

He struggled and thrashed, but the stasis-afflicted soldiers didn't budge.

"Little help here?" he called out, addressing the ceiling. He'd never used magic outside the timeline before.

The room's chrono didn't move. 0602, military time. Just after six in the morning on a day where maybe he ought to have slept in.

Closing his eyes, the Village of Eternity was inaccessible.

Oh, Eric had really done it this time.

Would he die of starvation if he had to wait five years for this life-sized diorama to return to normal?

Would he go mad?

Five years was a long time to do nothing, go nowhere, speak to nobody. And he could have an arm go numb sleeping on it wrong for half an hour. The statuary grip on his upper arms would render blood flow to his upper extremities a problem long before hunger, thirst, or fatigue set in.

He couldn't stay like this. Not for five years. Not for a day.

Things need to move a little. Speed this up.

Almost imperceptibly, the briefing room returned to motion. But it was more a feeling than anything his eyes could perceive.

Heaving, he was able to pull an arm free. He felt bones crack and heard muscles tear, but he left that problem to doctors in the distant future. With the extra leverage partial freedom afforded him, breaking the fingers of the second hand went quicker.

Eric heaved a sigh of relief, noticing that his movements were all sluggish. It felt like wading through a pool, except the water was pancake syrup.

Pancakes.

Eric promised himself a week of nothing but pancakes if he managed to get out of this alive and intact enough to feed himself.

The exit was blocked by bodies. A nudge was all it took, but Eric was a bullet ricocheting through the crowd. His touch was a hammer blow, his shoulder a tram car.

Out in the hallway, security doors blocked the way out of the bunker. A swift, sharp kick not only knocked one door out of its slidey track in the floor, it set the edges of the door melting like a ship entering atmosphere too fast.

Mom used to do that to show off since, at just the right speed, the fire cleaned the outside of the ship without damaging the metal and glassteel.

Eric was determined to *see* Mom again. And Dad. And Jessie and Ozzy and Mort and Sparta and Harmony and Trebla and a whole lot of other people. But most especially Charlotte.

Never having been back outside the bunker, it took Eric a few missed turns to find his way first to a manual staircase, then the correct door to exit.

When he finally encountered sunlight, Mars had changed.

New Vancouver looked brighter and more trafficky than he'd remembered it. Several nearby buildings didn't match his memory of the bunker entrance. The New Vancouver Civic Center was undergoing massive construction.

Two red-uniformed guards carrying blaster rifles lined with arcane runes whirled on him.

"Who goes there?"

Where to begin? With too many lies swirling in his brain, Eric's mouth blurted the truth before someone pulled a trigger on one of those maybe-magic-won't-make-them-miss blasters aimed his way. "I know I don't look like it but I'm Eric Ramsey. I can explain everything, if you just—"

"Eric Ramsey?" the other guard echoed.

"Yeah." OK. Maybe this wasn't a horrible plan. Plan A's rarely went anywhere. It was usually K or later before Eric had anything remotely viable.

"If you're *really* Eric Ramsey, what's Eric Ramsey's favorite ice cream flavor?"

The question struck him a physical blow. Eric reeled. "How can I answer that? I didn't give you any kind of passcode for ice cream. And who did *you* get it from? I mean, the answer would be different if my mother or father gave it to you as opposed to Commodore Grosset. And if it was Charlotte, when did you talk to her, because I don't think I really hashed out my recent opinions regarding pistachio with her before coming to Mars, so—"

"It's him. Call it in. Inform Captain Ramsey that her brother finally emerged."

Eric's heart soared. They were Jessie's people. Or at least they were friendly with Jessie. But he had to know. "How could you be sure it was me?"

The guard who hadn't just opened a comm smiled. "We were told that the only person who wouldn't be able to at least *answer* that question would be the real Eric Ramsey."

———

Eric waited on a granite park bench with Rudy and Manuel, his new friends working for the Temporal Defense Division of the Martian Parks Service. Once they'd contacted the *Arete* and established an ETA of an hour and a half or so, the three of them had just started chatting.

Not quite three years. That's how long it had been since the temporal anomaly Eric had created. In the meantime, New Vancouver had cordoned off the area and established the Time (Im)memorial, a monument park dedicated to the failed coup that had briefly taken over Mars.

"So, you're *sure* the war is over?" Eric asked between sips of his Bonono-flavored Tropicola that Rudy had bought him from a nearby vending machine. When Eric had attempted to throw the occupants of the bunker ahead in time to escape them, he'd never envisioned the act would result in the nearby placement of vending machines.

"Over and done," Manuel confirmed.

Rudy slurped from his Eepple Tropicola, nodding before adding, "Good riddance. We're part of the League of Independent Planets now."

"Oh. How great!" Eric exclaimed. "It's like ARGO, but flipped around."

"Except for Earth," Rudy added. "They're still floating solo."

"Solo plus like sixty mid-core worlds and a few backward-ass border colonies," Manuel amended.

"Don't worry. With the League having our backs, they won't dare restart a war to reunify," Rudy explained, possibly reading the concern on Eric's features. Eric had put a lot of effort into matching his old features, using Manuel's powered-off datapad as a mirror, and he knew all too well how well it conveyed and how poorly it hid worry.

"Um. Who's in charge everywhere nowadays?"

"Hal got us a great deal joining the League," Rudy told him.

Manuel nodded and gave his partner a fist bump. "Ladenburg for the League. He won the special election after you took the dictator and his cronies off the table."

"You mean General Bob?"

"We don't like saying his name, but yeah, Bob Randall can rot in that time anomaly for all anyone cares."

Eric scowled. "Just in case, be ready for that all to end about five years from when I started it. I slogged through gooey, swampy time to walk out, but it was only supposed to be a five-year hiatus when I created it."

Rudy whipped out his datapad and set his Eeple Tropicola on the seat of the bench beside Eric. "I'll inform HQ. It'll be in my report, but I think that's something they oughtta know ahead, in case I get hit by a hover walking home."

As if on cue, a hover van pulled up nearby. The letters MNN were emblazoned across the side.

Manuel shook his head and elbowed his partner. "Damn. Someone caught wind."

"Guy's got his face on the north side of the monument. Without his disguise, it was only a matter of time."

"Is there a problem?" Eric asked.

"Depends. How you feel about aggressive, in-your-face interviews?"

Eric shrugged. "I can take them or leave them."

Half an hour later, Eric was coming out of Hair and Makeup. A production assistant led him onto the set of Red Sky At Night, Mars News Network's top evening fluffy news program.

A polite crowd applauded him. Eric acknowledged them with a static wave as he kept walking as instructed by the green-room people. The host, Dahlia Steinberg, positively glowed. The epitome of everything modern and fake and scientific about public life, she had plastic-smooth skin and silver hair.

Not silver like someone wanted to be polite about gray, but silver like she could camouflage herself diving into a drawer full of expensive flatware. Her eye shadow, lip tint, and nails all matched. Make a circle of a few dozen of her, and her smile could have landed starships at night.

"Wizard Eric Ramsey, welcome to Red Sky At Night." If Eric hadn't already been told the name of the show, it was also scrawled in giant script on the back wall of the set.

He took the leftmost cushion of a couch angled toward Dahlia's desk. "Thanks. When I started the day, I honestly wouldn't have guessed I'd be here in twenty tries." Much beyond twenty, Eric's guesses started getting random, and he'd had the darnedest luck coming up with some oddball right answers.

Like the time Jessie *had* just been snorting expired whipped cream canisters with her friends.

Or when he randomly guessed that Uncle Roddy was thinking of the number 151.

Or Dad asking him to guess the Squadron 33 1/3 encore at the Dark Moon, and not only had the band *gotten* a request for an encore that night, they had played *Ballroom Blitz*, which was a song Eric had never heard them play live before.

Clearly, he had a lucky streak.

Dahlia Steinberg didn't seem interested in asking about his guessing skills, however. "How's it feel to be with us here in the year 2595?"

"A lot like 2592, if I'm being honest. I'm glad to see Mars doing so much better."

"I don't know if anyone's had a chance to inform you, but you've been granted honorary Martian citizenship for your heroic sacrifice, dragging the traitors into your time anomaly."

"I hadn't heard." He turned to the camera. "That's so sweet of you guys. Thanks."

"Can you tell us a little about what's going on inside the anomaly? Were you able to experience time passing trapped in there?"

Eric twisted his lips and tried to frame this in a way that the thirty billion or so people expected to be watching might understand. "To me, it was August 26, 2952, this morning. I woke up early, impersonating one of the wizards assigned to protect the fancy, high-ranking dictator people. But they caught me, and I tried to send them all into the future, where there would be plenty of time to prepare for how to deal with them. But I got caught up with them. I took the whole bunker, not just the people who weren't me. I could move, but with everything else frozen, I had a hard time making my way out. While I spent maybe fifteen or twenty minutes weaving through a statue garden of people and knocking down closed doors, apparently two years and three hundred and eighteen days passed for everybody else."

"Amazing. I can't wait to hear all about life on the inside of the Time (Im)memorial..."

The interview only lasted maybe five minutes.

More polite applause trailed after him.

Eric imagined that he was in for a doozy of a debriefing by police, military, ministries, agencies, and every other manner of official.

But there was a shuttle waiting for him outside the MNN studios. Haathee in design. Cleaned. Polished. Tinted with stylized red lettering across the sides that identified it as *Arete Shuttle 1*.

With the ramp down, a pachyderm toot greeted him.

"Grosstet?" he called out. As if there were any other haathee around. Then again, it had been nearly three years. Maybe, at this point, there were others.

"I WON THE HONOR IN A GAME OF CHANCE.
WELCOME HOME, ERIC."

As he climbed the ramp into Grosstet's shuttle, a giddy grin
plastered itself onto Eric's face.

Home.

———

The *Arete* had changed. Eric could see that the instant the
shuttle's ramp had let him out into the hangar. It was like every
time visiting Duster's Dogfight Diner. Dad knew the owner, so
every tour, Squadron 33 1/3 seemed to swing through. And
every time, they'd have moved the machines, rearranged the
tables, or added something to the menu. But at its core, it was
still the same pub food and zoomy flying game.

The hangar had been separated into an actual landing yard
and warehouse, with Grosstet's shuttle parked in a prominent
position in the former. Makket's little fleet of grav sleds all
looked the same now instead of a junk drawer mishmash of
models. The warehouse was labeled in English, Kejathi,
eyndar, and haathee. Numerous safety and signage features
common to terrestrial landing yards made clear where people
did and didn't belong around the various idle vessels.

Eric hoped that *he* still belonged.

So many people.

A crowd cheered as Eric emerged. Familiar faces numbered
among them, sure. But so, so many new people of all different
species. Attempting to block those out, he focused on the two
who'd staked out prominent positions ahead of the throng.

"I was so mad at you for so long," Jessie said before
encircling him in a quick, crushing hug. She wore what he
could only imagine was a dress uniform. Smartly buttoned.
Stiff collar. Epaulets. Medals. Contrasting with the military

blue uniform, she wore a red cloth headband, tied in place with the tails drooping behind her, with the Atik mono-symbols for *Spirit, Fist,* and *Magic* subtly emblazoned in orange across the forehead. She wore her hair in a ponytail half a meter long, pulled high to poke out above the headband. While all the rest of the look was new, too, he was more surprised to find an expertly subtle cosmo tint job, like she'd actually learned how to apply it herself or had a cosmetologist on staff. The earrings she wore dangled to her shoulders in a string of planetary symbols that it took only a fraction of a second to realize represented the homeworlds of the species aboard.

"I missed you, too, even though it was a lot shorter for me."

Then, his sister released him, and she vanished, for the moment, from his thoughts.

Charlotte.

Eric's eyes misted as the two locked together in an embrace. "I'm so sorry."

"I'm proud of you," she told him, and her voice was music for his soul.

Without releasing one another, they slid apart, still clinging by the forearms. Eyes met, and Eric knew in an instant that he'd have some explaining to do about the not-quite-right body he was displaying right now. She'd always known him better than he'd known himself, and looking into his own eyes to get them just right creeped him out.

"You're as beautiful as ever."

"Three years may as well have been a decade," she sniped back playfully. "I've eight gray hairs and tint them away so you'd recognize me upon your return." He'd have recognized her in a laaku costume and datagoggles.

But she *had* changed. Minimally, but he knew her well, too. Like Jessie, she wore an updated *Arete* uniform bejeweled with medals he'd have to hear tales about someday. Black-tinted lips and nails, with dark eye shadow, lent an appearance of mourning. Her long, black hair glinted in the hangar's scientific light, in desperate need of a good braiding.

"We're having a reception in the Great Hall tonight," Jessie informed him. "It's... well, there've been some changes to the ship. I'm sure Charlotte can keep you from getting lost."

The crowd pestered with questions and well-wishes as the honor guard of the ship's two top officers escorted Eric to the lift. The only one whom Jessie acknowledged was Daphne, who awaited them by the control panel.

"Is he allowed to wander, or will he need supervision?" the azrin asked. Her uniform still bore the cutoff sleeves she used to wear—or not wear—previously, but she no longer carried a blaster. By her insignia, Eric could tell she was a Commander and worked in security, however. She also wore a headband that matched Jessie's.

"I take full responsibility for him," Charlotte declared. When Jessie simply gave a nod instead of contradicting her executive officer, the matter was settled.

"I assume you'll want to freshen up?" Jessie asked. "I can assign you quarters if you'd rather not go back to—"

Eric turned to his girlfriend in a panic. "Wait. What?"

"Captain, don't concern yourself. I've kept all Eric's things where he left them, minus some soiled garments that Logistics Support have long since cleansed and folded." She turned to him. "She was concerned that *my* feelings might have changed in the interim without wishing to say so outright." Charlotte addressed the captain: "They have not."

Eric let out a long breath, filled with tension.

"Though I have grown somewhat deprived of affection. And I've had a bit of a Penelope Complex as presumptuous suitors attempted to declare an early termination to what they viewed as mourning. Captain, I promise to return him in time for tonight's celebration. In the meantime, if I may be excused from my shipboard duties?"

Jessie snorted as the doors opened near their quarters. "I don't even know how to joke with you about what you two do next. Sure. Take your time. We're calling the banquet 1900 hours, so try not to be too fashionably late."

Charlotte thanked the captain and made the way to their room with Eric towed by the hand.

Only once inside did her demeanor change.

"Who were you, and what happened to the Eric I sent to Mars?"

Eric gulped. "I... uh... there was a mishap."

"A mishap? You've come back in some poor sap's body. Don't tell me your original is stranded in the anomaly."

"I... died."

"You what?"

"Well, the body that was mine died. I'm in this one. Everything seems OK. Well, everything but being dead. I'm still me. Same as Mort is still Mort, now that I think about it."

"*Is* Mort still Mort? You never met the man, I'd thought."

"Well, Mort is Uncle Enzio. I can vouch for that much. And you've seen him in Mortania, and the match is pretty good, so I'm going to go with a pretty confident 'yes' on that front."

"Who was this body?"

"A wizard named Rasmussen of Mars Circle, Order of Hypnos. I'd have mentioned it at the bookshop, but we were short on time."

Charlotte snorted. "No loss, there. Most of Mars Circle was exiled. The Convocation hunted many of them down."

"Aunt Tiffany?" Eric speculated.

"She's still Dictator of Earth. Apparently, she's running

things too efficiently for anyone to trust democracy to take back over."

"But wasn't her whole job—?"

"Yes, the irony is apparently lost on Earthlings. If she truly *was* good at her job, she'd have made herself obsolete long before now. And presently, hunting down traitorous Martian wizards is below her pay scale."

Eric coughed. "So, what else have I—?"

"Eric, is that body of yours sick?"

"Not 'sick.' It's more chronic."

"And you're wheezing like you swallowed a referee's whistle, now that we're somewhere quiet enough to hear. Well, don't let Mordecai catch you in this state."

"Why? Has he learned to heal with magic?"

Charlotte scoffed. "If only. No. He'd find you a new host body and manually stuff your mind into it."

Eric snickered. "Mort's pretty strong, but I'm—"

"No match for him. He's been ship's wizard a while now. I've gotten to know him rather well. He is affable, erudite, and a quick-witted conversationalist, but his word is law when it comes to the universe. The *Arete* is as safe as it's ever been, and largely thanks to him."

"I wouldn't mind seeing him. He around?"

Charlotte smirked. "Oh, he didn't enjoy the prospect of the hullabaloo in the hangar, but he and Sparta will be at the banquet tonight."

"Great."

"And *they* have a surprise for you."

"Mind spoiling it?" Eric asked with a grin. He'd rather hear anything from her, directly.

"They have a daughter, and a second child on the way. Don't mention anything about Sparta's appearance, and if you somehow must, *please* let it not be that she resembles a python that's swallowed a football."

"I promise. What's the daughter's name?"

"Erica The Brown."

Eric's eyes widened. "Awww..." He immediately headed for the door. "I know we're going to see them later, but—"

"Get back here at once."

Eric's feet stopped before he'd decided on a course of action.

"Damn near three years since I've touched you, including your pre-anomaly undercover work. And I'm not counting that liaison in Mordecai's company. We're having a nap, and two or three lifetimes before the banquet, and at least one of them in which we will be small furry creatures who sleep in a pile. I've had my bloody fill of not having you around. Understood?"

Eric narrowed his eyes. Even when it came to Charlotte, he knew he could be dense once in a while. "Are you... trying to propose to me?"

Charlotte paused in peeling back the blankets from an immaculately made bed. "Eric, dearest, don't be dreary. Marriage is all sex and children and joint banking privileges. We're ever so much beyond that already. Why regress? Now, strip out of those Martian rags and get over here. We're waiving the shower-before-bed rule this once, and I expect you to whisk me to the Village of Eternity before the smell of cigar smoke and cheap coffee makes me regret my haste."

Not five minutes later, as reckoned aboard the *Arete*, the two of them were kittens in a world of yarn.

━━━

The door to Jessie's quarters closed, and immediately, she unbuttoned her uniform jacket. While her brother's return had been a relief on a level she could barely describe, the fawning and reacquainting and current-events lessons had exhausted her remaining emotional reserves over the course of three hours' worth of meal courses, drinks, and desserts with a heavy influence of Eric's favorites.

Just seeing her brother with Charlotte struck a chord across her heartstrings.

Three years of separation, and they snapped back together like the opposite-poled magnets they both were. Jessie loved them both but couldn't grasp quite what it was either saw in the other.

Despite returning from the largest meal she'd consumed since the post-games spread following the Fourth Arete Games, she headed immediately for the nightly snack spread provided by the Hospitality Division. Ignoring the regenerative BioJerky and the strictly nostalgic Snakki Bars, the bags of jalapeno and mozzarella corn chips, the analgesic-rich Choco-Chews, and the I've-got-work-to-finish-before-bed EnerJuice selections, Jessie cracked a rice beer loose from its self-cooling six-pack plastic and took a long chug.

Eric.

What a kid...

She felt bad when he went missing and somehow worse for having him back.

Everything on the *Arete* had been running so smoothly. Well, it wasn't as if things didn't still go wrong; they just seemed to go less *cataclysmically* wrong. Mort took care of all the magic the vessel needed. And sure, she maybe got a little more sass from the older-than-he-looked wizard, but it wasn't anything she wasn't used to from dealing with Uncle Enzio growing up.

Jessie had a crew of three hundred eighty. She had department heads who could all but run the vessel without her.

Her missions came from requests of planetary governors, heads of state, megacorporate sponsors. And if she didn't like what they wanted from her, she could always just choose any task she liked, and her people didn't question her (much).

How was all that going to change with Eric back?

Midway through her second beer, and as she was meditating half a meter off the floor beside her minibar, her datapad chimed.

Putting her feet back into gravity's custody, Jessie walked over barefoot and retrieved her annoying link to the ship outside her quarters.

Yeah.

This was what she'd felt coming.

```
Captain Ramsey,


After considerable deliberation, I hereby
tender my resignation as first officer of the
Haathee Federation Vessel Arete. I have
appreciated my time in your service, and I
wish you all the best. While my
recommendation for a replacement would be
Commander Sedgwick, you are, naturally, free
to choose whomever you wish. However, her
experience at Tactical makes her an ideal
candidate to face the dangers you have always
willingly embraced.


As for your brother and me, we intend to make
our way in the galaxy, just the two of us.
There are adventures to be had and magics to
explore that would be best kept well clear of
the orderly operation of a vessel with such a
```

noble mission as the Arete. I make no
promises but fully intend that Eric and I
shall keep in touch well enough that you and
the remainder of your family need not fret
over our well-being.

Much love,
Wizard Charlotte Webber, Order of Morpheus

Jessie noted the distinct lack of mention of her own rank aboard the *Arete*. Setting aside her datapad, Jessie threw back the remainder of her rice beer.

One party down, she was going to have to throw a going-away version for her first officer.

But before that, she was going to need a new first officer.

Scooping up the datapad in one hand as she deftly popped the top on another beer with the other hand, Jessie started a new text comm.

Mindy,

Report to my ready room at 0800 hours. Don't mention anything to anyone but Daphne.

Jessie didn't sign her orders. And she didn't expect Mindy to keep the heavily-hinted-at promotion from her wife. It was an open secret that Charlotte was only sticking around for Eric to return. It sucked, as a sister, wishing that she could keep her efficient, unimpeachable, cool and collected first officer even if it meant Eric stayed lost in time until her retirement.

Well... it wasn't like the *Arete* didn't have enough mental health professionals aboard these days.

However, Jessie wasn't in the mood for personal growth and acceptance at the moment. Escapism took center stage as she worked her way quickly through a third beer and her second text comm.

Commander Chinochin,

Run the Captain's Lottery for me. Schedule for 2330 hours.

Jessie brought beer number four with her to the washroom and set it on a custom shelf within reach of the shower but shielded from the falling water. She had about an hour to decide how drunk and how awake she intended to be when 2330 rolled around.

After learning lessons about playing favorites with Lorenzo and Junior, Jessie had opened up her evenings' companionship to a random drawing. Anyone could enter. Everything was optional. She'd tried to keep an open mind, and only two crew members had been blacklisted from the lottery since its inception.

Command could be a lonely place, and Jessie resolved to be alone with someone else as often as she needed.

Amy waved from the back of the crowd, and Carl shot her a sly wink as he grooved. Throughout the remainder of *Magic Carpet Ride*, she flailed her arms like she lost a bet and had to dance to a song that was not, strictly, well suited for dancing. And—love her to death—Amy couldn't dance to save her life.

Luckily, it had never come to that.

As the final chords rang out, Carl flicked on his microphone. He noticed that Amy was still gesticulating. With a squint, he realized she was wagging a datapad. Instantly, Carl Who Was Going to Announce the Next Song In This Set swapped places with Carl Who Needed a Quick Five and Knew a Song That Didn't Need Him.

Because it took a lot for Amy to interrupt a live set.

Because there was only one reason Carl would take a comm that she couldn't handle solo.

"Here we go. Up next... an old favorite of my old man's... *Cat's In the Cradle*."

The rest of the band knew the drill. There were a dozen songs Carl could sneak out during. Often, it was a clue that he had too much to drink and either needed a piss or to puke. But whatever they imagined his reasoning was this time, Roddy and Jean kicked it into gear. By the time Yomin came in on vocals, Carl had his guitar in a stand offstage and was wending his way through the crowd.

When Amy headed for a side exit, Carl altered course to intercept.

Out in the alley beside the *Toasted Goat*, she mouthed, "(*It's Mort!*)"

Smirking like he was playing along with a gag, Carl accepted the datapad. Instantly, his face fell. She was serious. "Mort? The hell, man. What's up?"

"That boy of yours clawed his way free of that clock-cocoon he wrapped himself in."

"Eric's back?" Amy exclaimed, jostling to get on camera in the cramped alley and tiny datapad screen.

"No," Mort deadpanned. "I was referring to Oswald. Of *course* I mean Eric."

A high voice off-screen commented. "Yes. It's Gramma and Grampa. Hold on. Mort, can you...? Yeah. Thanks."

The wizard dodged aside and a toddler with chocolate on her face grinned and giggled.

"Hiiiii, Erica!" Amy cooed, waving to the baby. Then, she addressed Sparta. "God, she's getting so big."

"Focus, here," Mort interjected. "Yes, the stinky little goblin keeps growing despite my admonitions. Stop growing!

You're getting less cute by the minute! As for your grown son, the one missing since founding a temporal tourist trap—"

"We're still looking for kickbacks from that," Carl commented.

"He's not only back aboard the *Arete*, but we just finished stuffing him full of flapjacks and shitty processed science cakes."

"Mort! Language!"

Without missing a beat, he addressed his wife. "I will teach that fairy sprite every horrible word she'll ever need in due course. The earlier she starts with the basics, the better. As for Eric—*if I may continue uninterrupted*—he and that honorary daughter-in-law of yours are already planning on a departure."

"Is he all right?" Amy asked. "Did he eat enough in the time anomaly?"

"I don't know that he was gone long enough to get hungry," Mort countered. "But they're taking a ship in the morning. Don't know that they've decided which one. We're a damned used hover lot down in the hangar these days. But I'll get someone to send you a way to contact them."

"Where they heading?" Carl asked. "Do they have a place picked out?"

"Not the foggiest. Doubt they've thought that far ahead. Thought maybe if you wanted to be on the itinerary, you could arrange something *tout de suite*."

"Who's piloting them?" Amy asked.

Sparta leaned into the frame again, and Erica waved. "Charlotte's been practicing. By her own word, she's as good as Wizard Tiffany by now."

Carl and Amy exchanged a knowing look. That wasn't saying much.

"Thanks for the heads-up. How're things your way?" Carl asked.

"Oh, same old," Mort replied with a shrug. "Our second's due in a couple months."

"Eddie," Carl blurted. "Assuming it's a boy. If it's a girl..."

"It's a boy," Sparta revealed. "Please don't make the joke asking how I know. And his name will be Troy."

"Troy The Brown?" Carl inquired with a grin.

Mort harrumphed. "Naturally."

"All right. Gonna let you go. My band's up on stage, and they need me."

Mort cackled. "Just tell me to fuck off. No need to *lie* about it."

The comm ended. The screen went blank. Carl turned to his wife. "They *do* need me. Right?"

Amy shoved the datapad into his hands. "Comm our daughter. Find out the registry and ID for whatever ship Eric and Charlotte are taking."

Captain Jessica Ramsey no longer felt like a polite fiction. Her ready room could have belonged aboard the finest corporate vessels and would have been the envy of any captain or admiral in any of the major galactic navies. It fit her like an old boot. Walls displayed her trophies, from a collection of eyndar pilots' helmets to a rack of assorted pirate blasters, but more precious were the plaque and flatpic from the Ghenlar Par'Mol refugees in their new home on Garrelon, the shell imprint from Uom'pe's great-great grandchildren, taken after her funeral, and the Inpok of Nelray Science Award in Medicine, shared jointly with Dr. Harmony Richelieu and Grosstet, for the advent of a new age in medical science.

It hadn't been some Earth Navy lieutenant who'd impacted so many lives.

Today, she'd borrowed a portable drill from her Engineering staff and was just finishing mounting two certificates behind her desk. One had been given to her by the Dictator of Earth personally, just weeks ago, and had been awaiting its partner. Freshly unpacked from a special governmental crate emblazoned with the logo of the League of Independent Planets, it joined Earth's version.

Each proclaimed Jessica Judith Ramsey as Ambassador to the Haathee Federation.

The door chimed, and Jessie forced herself to remember that her first officer was Mindy Sedgwick now. In the days since the promotion, she'd only slipped up once, but calling her Webber in front of the whole bridge crew had taken a couple beers after shift to smooth over.

"Come on in."

Her precaution was in vain.

"YOU WISHED TO SPEAK TO ME?"

Jessie gave the League certification a quick eyeball, knowing that if she got it crooked enough, someone from Logistics was bound to sneak in and adjust it while she was elsewhere aboard the *Arete*. Deciding it was good enough for now, she spread a hand toward the haathee-sized guest chair that only he and the stuunji crew members used.

"Eric's safe. I think we've given him and Charlotte enough of a grace period to change their minds."

"I HAD HOPED THAT ERIC WOULD DECIDE TO RETURN. HIS JOY WAS SHARED TOO LITTLE AFTER SO LONG AN ABSENCE."

"It's his joy," Jessie countered. "He's choosing to share it with Charlotte, and she was pretty clear that whatever he wanted to do when he emerged from the anomaly, she was doing it with him."

"THEY WOULD MAKE WONDERFUL PARENTS."

"Not that kind of doing it."

Grosstet let a toneless breath exhaust through his trunk. "ALAS."

Not wanting this meeting to turn maudlin, Jessie stood and made several noises she'd practiced and played back on recordings until she was convinced it was good enough.

Grosstet cocked his head. "YOU... WISH TO GO TO A PARAKEET AUCTION?"

Jessie tried again.

The haathee scowled. "MY GRANDMOTHER DID NO SUCH THING!"

Realizing he'd understood her just fine, Jessie couldn't help laughing. "Do you want to visit home or not?"

The mirth faded into undisguised sincerity. "I DO. ARE YOU CERTAIN YOU ARE WILLING? THE DISTANCE IS VAST."

Jessie smirked as she slid back into her desk chair. "Galaxy's smaller than you think." She keyed an internal comm. "Mort, you there?"

"Confound it, Jessica. Bad enough this gremlin refuses to use a toilet. I don't need you yammering after me while I chase a squealing manure thief around my quarters."

She'd suggested many a time that he use magic to wrangle Erica. But apparently there was a way things were done, and magic was strictly meant to awe and delight a child until age ten or so, at least if they were to fall in love with the arcane and want to learn it professionally.

"How long would it take us to get to the Haathee Federation?" This wasn't a question out of the black. They'd gone over maps and charts, and even dragged poor Aunt Shoni in for a conference comm to consult.

Mort grunted. *"Depends. If you're willing to taste numbers and experience a millennium or so as a ham sandwich, I could possibly have us there in time for dinner."*

Grosstets little eyes widened. It was so rare to see the whites around his irises. "ASSUME WE ARE NOT."

"Well, if you're OK with astral the color of clotting blood, let's call it a couple weeks."

Jessie spread her hands. She knew the haathee's animated facial expressions well enough by now to tell he was shocked. "(Surprise)," she whispered.

"I... OH, MY... WEEKS? IT TOOK DECADES TO MAKE IT THIS FAR. THIS IS A JOKE?"

"I wouldn't joke about this," Jessie swore. "We use the stardrive so we don't become reliant on Mort's magic for all travel. And because the nav computers, comm array, and omni connections on every device aboard hate it. But for a special trip like this... I think it's time to see what magic like Eric's can really do in the hands of someone who knows how to control it."

"If this isn't all hypothetical, can you order Sparta to change her daughter's diaper?"

"Far be it from me to interfere in the division of marital chores," Jessie replied. "Report to the bridge when you're done." She ended the comm before any harrumphing spoiled the mood.

"THIS WILL REALLY HAPPEN?"

"Erica's squirmy and quick, but she won't outrun Mort for long."

"I MEAN GOING HOME."

"My home is the stars. We've been to the homeworlds of most of the crew by now. I think it's time we *all* got to see where our commodore and our ship came from."

Grosstet's ears flapped involuntarily. "OH MY. I

IMAGINE THE *ARETE* MUST BE SO OUT OF DATE. I HOPE THEY STILL MANUFACTURE SPARE PARTS."

That was about the time that Jessie remembered that this ship was a century old. Human and laaku science were so far behind the *Arete* that its emergency med kit won them the Inpok of Nelray Science Award. She could only imagine the prizes to be won after a shopping trip to the haathee equivalent of a Cheapo Depot.

One of the perks of having a sister with her own giant starship was getting to take one of the little ones parked inside it without being asked for a security deposit. Even better was the option to rename it prior to flying out and into the great big Black Ocean.

Now, Eric and Charlotte watched the stars laze past as they occupied the two front seats of the *Tempestuous Play*.

A sudden giddiness overcame Eric, and he shook his fists in front of him, teeth clenched in a smile. "It's just us. We can do whatever we want. Go wherever we want. BE whoever we want." His exuberance triggered a small fit of coughs, quickly brought under control.

"About that. I can understand you took that body of convenience, and you've made it look *ever* so close to your original. But it's a shabby, rotted thing you'd do well to replace."

"I know..." Eric whined. "But it'll be fine for a while. Spare bodies aren't just lying around all over the place."

Charlotte lifted one eyebrow.

"You know what I mean!"

Charlotte sighed in admission that she did, in fact, know. "You were cheated of a body. Whether by accident or design, it matters not. You are an adjunct hero of Mars. And your reward is the walking carcass of a wizard who ought to have appreciated his mortal flesh more and his studies, perhaps, a touch less."

Eric slouched in his seat, watching Charlotte's hands control their flight. "Yeah. But it's not like I can file an insurance claim for a new body. And I don't know if I can trust science enough to let it fix me."

"That leaves us two options."

"Option one?" Eric asked, playing along. She could have just started listing them, but she liked the interactivity of being asked.

"We find ourselves competent magical help. Earth is the likely source of someone who can put that wracking cough and those aching bones to right. Is there anything else you're hiding?"

"Milk sits in my stomach like a grade-school science volcano."

Charlotte shook her head, and he could practically see the jotting of that fact onto a list on parchment in the bookshop of Charlotte's mind "I encourage you to give thought to the less obvious ailments and maladies that lie yet uncovered in your rental corpse."

"What's my second option?" Eric asked sullenly. This trip was already sounding like less fun than he'd hoped.

"We make our overarching adventure a quest to populate the Village of Eternity. I think we've established conclusively that its existence is *not* tied to the body you've discarded. You being able to reach my bookshop through Mortania, I think, suggests that it may not be a *place* at all. Or at least not a place you're carrying around with you. And if you can hold multitudes of souls in trust, I think it's your duty—our duty—to see that the lives therein are both plentiful and rich."

"You mean... more variety of minds to learn from?"

"Precisely."

"And how do you propose we do that?"

Charlotte focused her attention pointedly on her flying, even though they were in the middle of nowhere and out in realspace. "I daresay that we'll need access to people we can disposition at our discretion without drawing undue attention from forces that might object to your admittedly murderous beneficence."

"You're not suggesting we start a religion...?"

"No. You've got quite enough worship from those already cooped up in the infinite space you've carved out of the universe. No, I think we need people who'll accept your judgment as law and the occasional murder or disappearance as an operating cost of business."

Eric's brow furrowed, and he tried to figure out why. "Who would let us be that?"

"Eric, have I shown myself to be a hypocrite?"

"Not really..."

"What if I told you that the circumstances of a vow can change its relevance?"

"I think there's precedent," Eric replied warily.

"Because I've a way that I think solves all our problems, but it involves backtracking on a stated life goal and recanting a vow made in anger."

"Should I be worried? I'm starting to worry."

"We've talked about doing real good in the galaxy, and I think that reforming miscreants wholesale could be a way to go about that. Remove evildoers from the world we're in presently and reforge that villain program of yours into something grander and more deliberate."

"A... De-Villainization Factory?"

"We'll work on a name. But I think the clearest place to

start will be to apologize to my mother and rejoin the Poet Fleet."

Eric's eyes went so wide that he worried his eyelids might get stuck inside his skull.

"This is the reaction I expected. But hear me out."

"Your mother is *mean*."

"Indeed. It may be her most defining characteristic, though I'd call it spiteful."

"And nasty."

"You're being redundant."

"And... and... I think a lot of the people who work for her *like* having her in charge."

"Yes, but they've had it hammered into their craniums— possibly even literally, in some cases—that I am her proper heir. And... well... there has been a recent addition to the family. Since I'm not going to condone any harm to a three-year-old, we'll take responsibility for raising my sister once I've replaced my mother as admiral."

"But you didn't *want* to be admiral!"

"I still don't. But I think, as a means to an end, we can play pirates a while. Oh, evil will be done in our names, but you can't halt a screeching tram simply by snatching up the rail. We'll ease them out of the business."

"Like pruning a poisonous plant?"

"Until it withers."

"How did you end up with a sister?" Eric was struggling not to lose track of the details.

"Oh, my contacts in the fleet were cagey. Call it dark science and leave it at that."

Somehow, this all sounded optimistic. After last time, Eric didn't see how they'd be *allowed* back aboard the *Look Upon My Works Ye Mighty and Despair*, let alone welcomed.

Eric stared out the windows. "Can't we just pick any of those stars and be... us?"

"The ship's launched on your being you. Part of the appeal of this plan is picking out a better body for you. Maybe even for me, if we get ambitious."

Eric whirled in his seat. "You're perfect the way you are!"

Charlotte cupped his cheek in one hand. Her skin was warm and soft. "We can certainly gallivant off, be galactic vagabonds by day and frolic in the Village of Eternity by night. We can allow the Poet Fleet to continue its rampant run—"

"Jessie will stop them."

"She's got another mission in mind, far from Poet space. And she can't be the answer to all the galaxy's problems. But we don't have to be, either. We can allow the suffering of slaves like Margery, the malice of whatever wizard replaced Patroclus. We can let my mother raise another daughter as a pawn to be promoted after a forced march to the eighth rank of her life.

"Or we can take responsibility for unraveling the sins of my kin. I will flatly admit that I cannot do it without you, and I don't want to try. Say the word, and I'll never speak of this plan again."

Eric studied the hands clasped in his lap as they wrung together.

"We cannot go back in time to undo my childhood, but we *can* keep history from repeating."

Eric looked up, somber and serious. "What's her name?"

"Jane. Jane Austen Chisholm. She's recently turned three and will have no lingering memory of her mother unless she joins the Order of Morpheus in some distant year. She is, by all accounts, cute as a kitten and quite precocious. I think... minus the onus of having to conceive and bear one ourselves, we'd... well, I think you'll make a wonderful father."

"You really think so?"

"I know so."

This wasn't the sort of thing that could get a definitive answer. Eric gulped and nodded. "Let's do this. Let's go find a thread of yarn to tug on until the whole crocheted pirate blanket unravels. Let's be parents for a while. Let's find me a new body from someone who *really* doesn't deserve to have it."

"Excellent. I've already begun formulating the basics of a plan. To get close to Mother, we'll need to work our way inward. I think targeting an outlying fleet captain, we can get ourselves captured and work from within. We'll make a rollicking, old-fashioned, multi-stage heist of it."

Eric grinned. THAT sounded like fun. Reaching into a pocket, he pulled out a spoon.

"What's that? Did you rob the *Arete's* kitchen before we left, or did you simply collect it like a magpie and forget to return it?"

Eric dropped the spoon to clatter on the floor of the *Tempestuous Play* between their seats.

"What was that all about?"

"For luck. I'm pretty confident this plan is going to work."

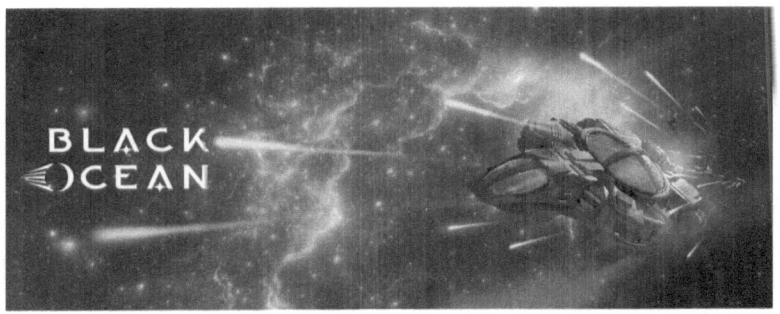

Black Ocean

Black Ocean is a vivid 26th century story universe where science and magic coexist—sort of.

Black Ocean: Galaxy Outlaws (16 missions)

Black Ocean: Galaxy Outlaws is a fast-paced fantasy space opera series about the small crew of the *Mobius* trying to squeeze out a living. If you love fantasy and sci-fi, and still lament over the cancellation of *Firefly*, *Black Ocean: Galaxy Outlaws* is the series for you.

Read about the *Black Ocean: Galaxy Outlaws* series and discover where to buy at: galaxyoutlawsmissions.com

Black Ocean: Astral Prime (12 missions)

Co-written with author M.A. Larkin, *Black Ocean: Astral Prime* hearkens back to location-based space sci-fi classics like *Babylon 5* and *Star Trek: Deep Space Nine*. *Astral Prime* builds on the rich *Black Ocean* universe, introducing a colorful cast of characters for new and returning readers alike. Come along for the ride as a minor outpost in the middle of nowhere becomes a key point of interstellar conflict.

Read about the *Black Ocean: Astral Prime* series and discover where to buy at: <u>astralprimemissions.com</u>

Black Ocean: Mercy for Hire (16 missions)

Black Ocean: Mercy for Hire follows the exploits of a pair of do-gooder bounty hunters who care more about saving the day than securing a payday. The series builds on the rich *Black Ocean* universe, centering on a couple of fan-favorites and introducing a colorful cast for new and returning readers alike. Fans of vigilante justice and heroes who exemplify the word will love this series.

Read about *Black Ocean: Mercy for Hire* and discover where to buy at: <u>mercyforhiremissions.com</u>

Black Ocean: Mirth & Mayhem (16 missions)

Black Ocean: Mirth & Mayhem delves into the origins of two vagabonds making their living among the stars. Mort is a wizard coming to grips with a life on the run and estrangement from the comforts and respect he had on Earth. Brad is an impressionable youth, too clever for his—or anyone's—good. And Chuck Ramsey is the mold that Brad's trying to break out of, which is harder than he could ever have dreamed.

Read about *Black Ocean: Mirth & Mayhem* and discover where to buy at: <u>mirthandmayhemmissions.com</u>

Black Ocean: Passage of Time (in-progress)

The year was 2586. A few minutes later, it was 2591. Caught up in a time travel snafu, Eric and Jessie Ramsey become fugitives from the people who want answers as to how they did it—and where their loyalties lie in the galactic war that broke out in their absence.

Read about *Black Ocean: Passage of Time* and discover where to buy at: <u>passageoftimemissions.com</u>

Black Ocean Fan Group

Join the *Black Ocean* Facebook fan group to discuss *Black Ocean* with other outlaws. Chat about ebooks, audio, or paper versions; main series or spin-offs; or share photos of the pet you named after Kubu.

Request to join at: blackoceanfans.com

Black Ocean Merch

Wish you could live in the Black Ocean world?

I can't promise you'll win an argument with the universe, but you CAN wear your own wizard hoodie (adorned with Convocation medallion), disguise your boring 21st-century soda or beer with the Earth's Preferred can cooler, or fly the Poet Fleet Jolly Roger.

Browse merch at: blackoceangear.com

Twinborn Chronicles

The *Twinborn Chronicles* is an epic fantasy saga based on the possibility that our dreams offer us a glimpse into the life of another – another who can get the same glimpse into our world.

Read about the *Twinborn Chronicles* and discover where to buy at: twinbornchronicles.com

Twinborn Chronicles: Awakening

Experience the journey of mundane scribe Kyrus Hinterdale who discovers what it means to be Twinborn—and the dangers of getting caught using magic in a world that thinks it exists only in children's stories.

Twinborn Chronicles: War of 3 Worlds

Then continue on into the world of Korr, where the Mad Tinker and his daughter try to save the humans from the oppressive race of Kuduks. When their war spills over into both Tellurak and Veydrus, what alliances will they need to forge to make sure the right side wins?

Project Transhuman: Eve14

Project Transhuman brings genetic engineering into a post-apocalyptic Earth, 1000 years aliens obliterated all life.

These days, even the humans are built by robots.

Charlie7 is the oldest robot alive. He's seen everything from the fall of mankind at the hands of alien invaders to the rebuilding of a living world from the algae up. But what he hasn't seen in over a thousand years is a healthy, intelligent human. When Eve stumbles into his life, the old robot finally has something worth coming out of retirement for: someone to protect.

Read about all of the *Project Transhuman* books and discover where to buy at: projecttranshuman.com

OTHER BOOKS BY J. S. MORIN

Sins of Angels

Co-written with author M.A. Larkin, *Sins of Angels* is an epic space opera series set 3000 years after the fall of Earth. With the scope of *Dune* and the adventurous spirit of *Indiana Jones*, it delivers a conflict that spans galaxies and rests on the spirit of brave researcher Professor Rachel Jordan. Follow the complete saga, and watch as the fate of our species hangs in the balance.

Read about *Sins of Angels* and discover where to buy at:
sinsofangelsbooks.com

Shadowblood Heir

Shadowblood Heir explores what would happen if the writer of your favorite epic fantasy TV show died before the show ended—and the show was responsible. If you wonder what it would be like if an epic fantasy world invaded our world, this urban fantasy story might give you that glimpse.

Read about *Shadowblood Heir* and discover where to buy at:
shadowbloodheir.com

EMAIL INSIDERS

You made it to the end! Maybe you're just persistent, but hopefully that means you enjoyed the book. But this is just the end of one story. If you'd like reading my books, there are always more on the way!

Perks of being an Email Insider include:

- Inside track on beta reading and advance review copies (ARCs)
- Access to Inside Exclusive bonus extras and giveaways
- Best of my blog about fantasy and science fiction topics

Sign up for the my Email Insiders list at: jsmorin.com/updates

ABOUT THE AUTHOR

I am a creator of worlds and a destroyer of words. As a fantasy writer, my works range from traditional epics to futuristic fantasy with starships. I have worked as an unpaid Little League pitcher, a cashier, a student library aide, a factory grunt, a cubicle drone, and an engineer—there is some overlap in the last two.

Through it all, though, I was always a storyteller. Eventually I started writing books based on the stray stories in my head, and people kept telling me to write more of them. Now, that's all I do for a living.

I enjoy strategy, worldbuilding, and the fantasy author's privilege to make up words. I am a gamer, a joker, and a thinker of sideways thoughts. But I don't dance, can't sing, and my best artistic efforts fall short of your average notebook doodle. When you read my books, you are seeing me at my best.

Connect with me online
jsmorin.com

facebook.com/authorjsmorin
bookbub.com/authors/j-s-morin
youtube.com/@authorjsmorin